Hear me Feel me

Ann Axisa

Published by YouWriteOn.com, 2011

Copyright © Ann Axisa

First Edition

A CIP catalogue record for this title is available from the British Library.

I would like to dedicate this book to my brother in law Anthony Grech.

Who after suffering with acute pancreatitis and two heart attacks followed by a stroke is a deep inspiration to me.
His bravery is unique, and I love him very much.

Good luck Tony for your future recovery.

Chapter One

Did she believe in ghosts?

This occupied Laura's mind from morning to night. She felt as though someone was watching her all the time ... thought she was hearing things: noises, and her name being whispered. Soft warm breaths landing on her face or neck even though the windows were shut. Making a fist, she pushed it hard to her mouth as she crossed her legs in fear that she would wet herself. Maybe she was going mad. They say losing somebody could send you barmy. After visiting the bathroom, Laura tried to calm herself. She laughed aloud, but a hollow sound erupted from her mouth then she spoke to her reflection in the mirror: *You silly cow, you're barmy, first sign of madness and all that.* She put her hair up in a ponytail and grabbed her coat. A shiver vibrated through her, and goose bumps were settling on her arms. It was the end of April and still chilly in the morning, although the spring sunshine was warm if there was no wind, but she knew the weather wasn't causing the chill seeping through her skin.

Laura made her way downstairs. All the food was prepared. She glanced at the sad *vol au vents* and the limp sausage rolls. She wiped her eyes, sore from all the crying she had done, and went to find Mia in the conservatory.
Family and friends were scattered around the house and garden. Some stood huddled under a large garden heater, smoking, others drank tea and nibbled the light refreshments.

Laura and Mia sat looking out on a long garden edged with trees, rock plants and shrubs. The garden weaved like a snake with clusters of snowdrops chasing daffodils as if in a race, only stopping when the stepping-stones at the far end impinged upon their journey. Looking past the garden there was a large tree standing alone in the distant fields, as though left there for a punishment. Laura felt the loneliness of the tree and sensed the same solitude. Laura had loved the way the garden had sprung into life come March, and each morning she would wander out and see more protruding buds escaping the soil. The house was also beautiful, nestled in the corner of a small road on the edge of Rednal. Laura had the best of both worlds. It was only twenty minutes into the city and there were two local villages within walking distance. Now as she sat there everything looked as though it was made of plastic.

 In the summer, she would sit next to the wide conservatory doors until late at night, chatting with friends or her sister. Even these doors were too narrow to facilitate her grief. Laura shook herself and took one look at Mia – and her terrible pain overwhelmed her again. She didn't think there was any salt water left in her body, she'd cried so much. They both sat there with tears streaming down their faces. Mia put her head on Laura's shoulder. Laura placed her arm around her sister and felt her shaking. Today had been a terrible experience. No wonder she was feeling jumpy.

They had been to the funeral of their sister Bonnie, struck down by cancer at the age of thirty.

Family and friends passed photos around and talked about Bonnie's small son – a beloved child. Everyone had wondered and kept hinting about the father, but Bonnie had refused to reveal the identity. She wouldn't even tell her sisters. It was going to be hard for Sam without a mom or dad.

Laura had promised Bonnie that she and Mia would make sure Sam felt loved, and that he would remember her. Sam had moved in to live with Laura and her husband James, who was working away.

All the sisters were pretty girls. Laura picked up a photo of her sisters and reminisced. Bonnie had been the darkest one in the family: it always looked as though she had just walked out of a trendy hair salon. They never managed to get their hair to look like hers: it always seemed to shine. Her two sisters had been envious that her hair was so vibrant. Laura noticed in the photo how close her two sisters looked. Mia was gazing up at Bonnie her cute little face, button nose and hazel eyes full of love. Mia was the shortest of the three but very pretty. However, she was quick-tempered and not as easy-going like the other two.
Laura put the photo down and drifted out into the garden. They both wanted the day to be over so that they could mourn alone.

"There are only two of us left now," sniffed Laura. Mia sat on their grandfather's old wooden garden seat, quietly crying and picking leaves off the privet hedge. She had soon amassed a small pile of them on the lawn.

 "Talk about stating the obvious, you silly cow! Go and sit over there if you can't think of anything good to say."

Laura, shocked by this vitriolic outburst, opened her mouth to speak, then closed it again.

The girls spent a lot of time together. Laura and Mia although having deep affection for each other had always found it hard to communicate without tension building up; Bonnie was always the one who kept everyone together. Since childhood, she had been a happy soul who hated to argue – or to hear others arguing. "I can't believe she's not here anymore! Her personality was so strong. She should be here," Mia cried.

At that moment, Laura felt peculiar sensations.

Oh no, not again She shivered as warm breath teased her neck. It rippled on her skin and sent tremors all the way down to her toes. It unnerved her, and she put her hand up and gave her neck a vigorous rub. She had had this feeling before. She first felt it when she was washing up, the day after Bonnie died. For the last two weeks, while Bonnie was in the hospice, she had used up all her clean crockery. She had the choice of washing up, or buying more crockery ... reluctantly, she'd reached for the Fairy liquid. She had sent herself into a trance as the soft bubbles spread over her hands only coming round when she felt the scalding water on her skin.

Wiping the last plate a warm sensation tickled her neck and she reached with her fingers and touched the area. Within seconds warm wind caressed her neck like a noiseless hairdryer for just fraction of a second, spinning around she almost dropped the plate she was drying. Since then the bizarre experience had happened repeatedly, but she was too apprehensive to mention it to Mia.

What were these mysterious warm breaths? She was almost sure it was Bonnie, trying to tell her something from beyond the grave.

As she looked over her shoulder she saw Mia following her into the house, this might be the time to tentatively mention her experience.

"Bloody hell, Laura, she's only just died, and you're saying you can feel her! When you're dead you're dead, finished, in the soil, kaput ... so shut the hell up about being able to feel her! If that is the case, why can't I feel her? I mean, she was with me more than you were. We were closer in age, and we spent almost every day together." Mia was breathing fast, and she couldn't control her emotions now. She knew she had hurt Laura feelings. Her face betrayed her struggle to control her emotions. Tears gathered on her lashes.

 "Laura, I can't do this now. I just can't." With that, she turned on her heel and ran inside. Laura shoved aside the dart of pain. Why? Sadness washed over her. *Are we ever going to get along? Oh Bonnie I miss you.*

After a while, the sound of Mia's footsteps broke her thoughtful silence. Laura turned to see her sister standing there chewing her bottom lip.

"Laura, I know you were close to Bonnie, we all were ... but you had your husband, so I felt I was closer to her. We spent most evenings together ... so if anyone feels anything it should be me ... and if, like you say, she can communicate with us, then ... why can't I feel her?" Her tears welled up again and she ran inside, sobbing.

Laura was puzzled. That was Mia's way of apologising but she was saddened by what Mia had said. She could understand though why her sister was so upset. Both her sisters had been closer to each other than to her. After she married James, she'd been so absorbed in her own marriage that she'd seen less and less of her sisters, especially for the first eighteen months.

Now that James was working abroad she had grown apart from him, and she relied on her sisters more than ever. She had covered up her unhappiness for the last two years.

To be honest, Laura was glad each time James went back to France. He used to come home once a month, but in the last six months, he'd returned only twice saying he had too much work to get through. When he was home, she hardly saw him because he went visiting his family and friends. But he did put his wages in their joint bank account, and Laura could use her bank card whenever she needed money. The bills were paid by direct debit, so she had no worries there.

Over the last few months Laura had started getting together more with her sisters, having meals and shopping. She felt guilty, because when their mother had passed away, she'd promised her that they would stay close. Their mother had said that they should always love each other, and whoever came into their lives may hurt them some time, but they would always have each other to turn to.

Mary had made them promise to stay close and they had worked hard to stay closer, especially Bonnie and Mia. They had spent a lot of time together – even more so after their mom died.

"Oh mum why aren't you here? We need you so much."

Laura started thinking of their mom and subdued, she went in to find Mia.

"Mia, are you up there?" Mia replied, "I'll be down in a bit ... I just need some time alone."

Laura flinched as Mia's words tore through her, but she also felt *she* needed time alone. She wished everyone would go away so that she could sit and think of Bonnie.

When Mia appeared, Laura threw her arms around her.

"I love you so much"

"I love you too, I'm just feeling tetchy please ignore me"

They grabbed each other's hands and went to get a coffee.

*** *** ***

Chapter 2

Bonnie

As it happened, Bonnie had been looking down on them from the apple tree. Wondering around the grounds of the house and garden, she had found the ultimate place to gather her thoughts. The immense anger she felt coursed through her veins like a fast flowing river.

"I'm dead, truly dead, so why have I got feelings?" she hollered.

The Tuesday that she died, she felt as though she had been pushed out of her body. There had been a white mist she could not see through which swirled around her body like a spiral of light. "No" she shouted and tried to jump back into her body, but it was solid and would not accept her. She was as light as a feather. It was a fascinating state to be in but she wanted to be alive not dead.

For two days, she floated around her body while it remained in the hospice, and then she was left behind.

On the third day, someone was wheeled into her room, and she felt the woman's illness.

"Another one, *Oh my God*" she thought. The nurse was talking and she called the woman Gemma, so at least she knew her name. Bonnie remained in the room with Gemma by force, each time she tried to leave she found herself transported back, almost yo-yo style. Eventually she gave up and lay down next to her on the bed.

On the Monday morning, she had a weird sensation, as though she had been released, and as she looked up, she felt herself spinning through clouds of amazing Coloured lights with glistening orbs floating around her. She threw her arms around herself and kept repeating "No, no, no."

Watching her own funeral was eye opening, and now she was in total shock: she could not believe she was seeing all her friends and family react to her demise.

She'd been astounded at the volume of beautiful flowers brought to her funeral, and she loved the dark oak coffin with cerise and white lilies draped across it. She didn't like the one hymn at the service: she thought it was boring, and she'd never heard it before. "Whoever chose that?"

Bonnie snapped her head around to see if anyone heard her. She wasn't sure whether she was speaking or thinking her thoughts. No one looked her way. She sighed.   Looking around at the mourners, she felt herself sag, a cold feeling crept through her stomach, and the scene was terrible. Laura and Mia wouldn't stop weeping. Bonnie was trying to get their attention. The service had been a bit too long she thought, there had been beautiful music – except for that awful hymn. They'd played her favourite song for her going in, and it made people cry more. Seeing her cousin Claire she started waving to her, but no one took the slightest notice. At that point she realised that no one could see or hear her.

She felt as if there was an invisible cord around her, pulling her in all directions and it took all of her will to move at all, and that worried her. She put her head in her hands and screamed with frustration. She kept trying to move but found she couldn't go far, and every time she tried she found herself jerked back where she started. Feeling indescribably agitated Bonnie paced up and down until the last of the mourners left the chapel. Everyone had gathered around the flower station where all the wreaths were laid she started reading the condolences. A smile reached her lips when she read

"Good bye my friend, I will love you forever love Marie."

All the cards had wonderful messages on, and her heart swelled.

"Well I'm still here and that's where I'm staying," she said under her breath.

She stayed with her sisters the whole time – even in the car when they went back to Laura's house. Once there, Bonnie looked around her and felt isolated but calmness enveloped her and she hugged herself. Laura's house was lovely. She had purchased it from their mother six years ago when their mom had moved into a luxury flat. All the sisters felt at home here. Bonnie thought of the garden and the times herself and Laura had sat gossiping, and instantly found herself there. "Wow, that's amazing!" Her voice startled her. It did every time she heard herself, and for a tiny moment, she felt alive again. Gliding around the garden she hovered above her uncle, who was talking about her.

"What a lovely young woman she was, it's a bloody shame that's what it is."

"I never even saw you for two years," Bonnie said. She wished people knew what *she* knew now. They would act differently, and if she could go back, she would make time for everyone in her family.

She wandered about a little longer, and then sat on the apple tree swing watching everyone. She loved Laura's garden: the apple tree had grown with a step in it, and one of the branches hung low and an ornamental swing had been placed there, which you could swing on but not high. They had sat there many times, laughing, and gossiping. Now she felt lonely, and did not understand the feelings that were passing through her. Surely, she shouldn't have *feelings* if she was deceased. She couldn't understand why she felt so outraged. She curled her fingers under her legs and squeezed. She felt like hitting someone – surely that wasn't right.

Bonnie felt she had changed: she was a softie when she had been alive. Oh, she knew she had passed over, but she hadn't gone anywhere special, resentment coursed through her.

"Why the hell can't you see me, you stupid morons?" she shouted. She had tried her best to chuck an apple but she couldn't grab it, all she could do was blow on people – and apart from Laura, everyone ignored it, or couldn't feel it! With sorrow, Bonnie turned her face into the apple tree and let the ripples of desolation wash over her.

***

Laura looked around her: she was sure she just heard someone say "stupid moron". How dare they, on the day of her sister's funeral? Everyone in the garden seemed sad and quiet, and no one was arguing as far as she could see. Looking around the garden, she noticed the swing moving back and forth slowly and a feeling of apprehension and nervousness flowed through her. Her heart started beating like a drum and her hands started sweating. "I am going mad," Laura said under her breath as she went back in the house. Looking out of the window the swing was still. She sat down and closed her eyes for a moment.

Laura felt broken inside. She was the eldest

at thirty-two, then came Bonnie, thirty, and Mia was the baby at twenty-eight. They were closer: she realised this, and understood Mia's reaction. She was missing her so much.

The girls never expected Bonnie to go so quickly. Bonnie had only been in the hospice for two weeks, and the doctors said they thought she would have about six weeks left. However, they gave her a course of chemotherapy to try to give her more time. The chemo had made her ill, and the retching had made her hoarse. The vomiting had not stopped, even with the anti-sickness medicine. She had lost her hair, and had over fifty ulcers in her mouth. She had called a halt then and refused any more treatment. Bonnie told them both together,

"I know you all love me, but I have had enough. I will die anyway let us have some quality time together" "Ok" Laura said a lone tear fell and landed on her lip. Bonnie wiped it away.

The sisters had planned to spend every waking hour together for the next four weeks, or as long as it took, and that is what they had prepared for. They were going to be sharing the four weeks, talking and giving as much love as possible with the time they had left. The sisters were laughing and joking with each other on the Monday and planned an indoor picnic with Sam the following weekend. Bonnie stopped laughing for a moment and said, "This is how I want you to remember me, laughing and joking"

"Oh please let's not talk about it," replied Mia. "Come on Bonnie tell me about that doctor again, it's hilarious." Laura caught Mia's eye and slightly shook her head at her to warn her not to get maudlin.

 The next-day Laura and Mia were both shocked when a phone call had woken them at six thirty four am; it was the hospice saying Bonnie had passed away in her sleep.

The whole family, cousins and friends, had been devastated.

Laura sat contemplating. Whatever anyone said, she was not imagining this blowing that she felt. She went upstairs, locked the bathroom door, sitting on the edge of the bath, she twisted her hands together and took a deep breath, "Bonnie, if it is you, please find another way to contact me. It's doing my head in, all that blowing."

She giggled to herself. If anyone heard her, they would send for the doctor.

If Bonnie had been alive, she knew she would have laughed too. Laura flushed the toilet and went back outside to offer more tea and sandwiches, though she had made far too many.

***

"Well, can you believe it," Bonnie said, "I've just learnt to blow, and she wants something else ... if she had half a brain she would realise if I could do anything else I damn well would! And where's my little boy, that's what I'd like to know? Who have they given him to? I totally understand him not being allowed to go to a funeral, but they could have him now. They both promised to look after him between them."

Bonnie felt like she had a triple attack of PMT – as though her blood was boiling. She was fuming because she left too quickly. She thought she would have had more time, for proper arrangements to be made for her son. He was only three, and that broke her heart. Where was he? She just wanted to hold him and give him cuddles once again.

When her consultant told her there was nothing

they could do to treat her except a course of chemotherapy, which might give her more time, she was heartbroken. The cancer had been advanced. She had gone to the doctor, as soon as she started bleeding heavily. She'd suffered, or thought she'd suffered, from haemorrhoids, ever since she'd had Sam. That was what the doctor had told her, so she'd put down the pain and slight bleeding to piles. Well, it was the worst news ever, and now she'd had to leave him, she was infuriated. Her sisters wouldn't recognize her, she thought.

Bonnie had been easy-going and a peacemaker, she had never used bad language, not much anyway, or lost her cool.

Well, where had that got her, she thought – not even alive, that's what! Well, she would have to try other ways to contact her sisters.

   Bonnie watched from a distance. She thought, "Poor Mia can't understand why I couldn't blow on her. I did try, but it only worked on Laura." She saw Laura bringing out a tray of tea so went up close and concentrated. She built up an imaginary energy, which travelled from her toes to her mouth and, in her normal voice, spoke in Laura's ear.

"Where's my Sam?"

The tray went up in the air, and six mugs of hot tea went flying, luckily missing everyone. Mia had just come down, as it happened. She cried out, "Are you ok, Laura? I'm so sorry I snapped at you, I really am. Please forgive me, and come and sit down. Whatever happened?"

Laura turned, grabbed a tea towel, and was dabbing at her trousers while holding the material away from her skin. She followed Mia into the back room while the cousins cleared up the mess. Laura, having turned deathly white, told her that she had heard Bonnie asking for Sam. Mia went to say something, but Laura put her hand up.

"Please listen to me, Mia; I think I'm going mad." She explained to her about the blowing, and how often it happened, and she told her about going to the bathroom and asking Bonnie to show her some other way of contacting her. Mia listened, but refused to believe her. In fact, she tried hard not to laugh at what Laura was telling her.

"Are you sure it's not the shock of losing her? Or your emotions just playing you up?" Laura looked at Mia, stunned.

"No it's not my emotions! It was her! She wants to see Sam and she is going to haunt me until she gets him. Look, I'm going to fetch him from Marie's – I'll be back in fifteen minutes, so hold the fort. See if you can get everyone to go home, if you can, ok?"

"Ok, don't be long then," replied Mia, still shocked.

Once Laura had left, Mia went into the toilet and laughed to herself. She was sure that Laura was on the brink of a breakdown. She grabbed some tissue to wipe away the tears. "Oh well, Bonnie, if you're around that's the first laugh I've had since you died." Mia flushed the toilet and went outside to try and get everyone to leave. She was glad Laura had a downstairs loo, otherwise fifty people up and down the stairs would be a nightmare – plus it had been her hiding place when things got too much over the last hour.

**

Laura arrived at Marie's. Marie was happy to have had Sam. Marie's mother had watched him for her while Marie had attended the funeral. Marie put her arms around Laura and gave her a hug. She thought Laura was looking traumatised because of the funeral.

"Do you want me to keep Sam longer? I don't mind, really."

No, I want him to come home now. I need to be able to see him and touch him. A tear rolled carelessly down Laura's cheek and Marie held her for the briefest of moments before Laura's head jerked up.

"I love you Marie"

"I love you too Laura"

"Marie thank you for having him. I'll catch up with you soon, I promise."

"You just look after yourself Laura, and remember I'm here if you need me."

"Thank you – I couldn't wish for a better friend! I'll ring you soon."

Sam was whooping with joy when he saw Laura. "Am I coming to your house, Auntie Lar?" He was never able to say "Laura", so "Aunty Lar" had stuck.

"Yes, darling, Auntie Mia is waiting for you." His face lit up. He loved his aunties very much. He didn't understand very well about his mummy, but he knew she was with the angels.

He only ever spoke about Bonnie at night, when he was tucked up for the night: then all the questions would come.

"Bye bye Maria thank you for the chocolate"

"You're welcome darling, I'll see you soon." Laura took Sam and was back in ten minutes. Some people were just putting their coats on and giving their best wishes, and two of the cousins were chatting to Bonnie's friends. Mia had managed to persuade everyone to go, saying they needed time on their own. Everyone went happily. Passing around photographs for the last two hours had people feeling despondent.

Laura was bothered now: her mind was in turmoil. She thought to herself, "I've just lost my sister and gained a son, and I'm also hearing Bonnie talking to me." Agitated she watched Sam running up and down the garden, and tears came to her eyes. He was so small and innocent. He deserved to have his mother. Life was so unfair! Laura turned and grabbed a tissue. As she wiped her eyes, she heard in her ear.

"That's my boy."

"For God's sake!" Laura shouted, and nearly

took her eye out with the tissue; she turned this way and that, her eyes darting around in every direction. She then heard a giggle, and she knew she wasn't mistaken – it really was her sister.

Laura sat down, speechless. She looked everywhere, expecting to see Bonnie. She looked in each corner, but saw nothing out of the ordinary. She sat quietly for a moment, then Bonnie whispered in her ear, "Tomorrow, when you wake up, take Sam to nursery and come back with Mia. I need to talk to you both. I'll come to you at 10 a.m. sharp."

Laura tried to stand, then sat back down. She was shaking from head to foot. "Damnation!" she said to herself. "I've got myself an appointment with the dead." Laura's mouth was opening and closing, but she couldn't make a sound. She closed her mouth and tried to make sense of all this: she knew now it wasn't her imagination, but she wasn't sure if she was ill or not. She stayed there for a further ten minutes, then rose to go and find Mia. As she got up she said out loud, "Very well, sis, I'll see you tomorrow – and don't you dare be late!"

CHAPTER 3

The next morning, Laura was wondering if she was going mad, or imagining things: had she really made a date with her dead sister? When she had told her, Mia also wondered if Laura had lost her mind. She didn't believe in ghosts or the afterlife, but she had also seen what Laura was like the day before. She started to think that maybe Laura was telling the truth – but then, on the other hand, she may be having a breakdown. "Well, we'll see about that tomorrow," she thought.

Mia didn't say anything to Laura. She didn't want to interfere, but she thought her husband James was vile and selfish for not wanting to be with her through this devastating time. If he'd been here supporting her, this breakdown or imagination problem might not be occurring.

She showered and dressed, then walked round to Laura's. It was only a ten-minute walk, and she was there for 8.30. They were lucky to all live within walking distance of each other. Sam was taking ages to eat his breakfast.

"Come on, Sam – eat up, you're going to

nursery in a minute: you'll be late."

"I've finished, Auntie Mia," Sam said, looking down at a full bowl of Coco Pops. "Come on, darling – eat up, and I'll get you a surprise later, when I pick you up."

"What surprise?" said Sam.

"Well, it wouldn't be a surprise, would it, if I told you – now, would it?"

Sam resumed eating, and finished in record time. Mia took him in her car to the nursery, which was a few miles away, and she was back in twenty minutes. "Right then, Laura, let's have a cup of tea and wait for the visit." She was laughing at Laura. Laura knew this was a wind-up, and she hoped Bonnie would speak to them and not make her a laughing-stock. She had thought while she was in bed last night that she was imagining things; and she'd decided she would need to see her doctor if nothing happened today.

At ten o'clock, the girls were sitting on the sofa, drinking tea and waiting. Laura was anxious, and Mia had a smug look on her face. Bonnie was standing by the window, watching them, wondering why Laura could hear her but Mia couldn't. She drifted behind Laura and whispered, "I'm here." Laura shot up, then sat down quickly.

"For God's sake, stop making me jump!" Mia also jumped.

"What are you saying, Laura, that Bonnie is here?" Laura looked at her and nodded slowly. Mia was spooked and felt a shiver vibrate through her.

"Ok, ask her to tell you something you wouldn't know, but I would." Mia stuttered. Bonnie pondered this, and before Laura opened her mouth, she said.

"Tell her about the fourth of June last year."

Laura repeated this, and Mia went white.

Mia said, "Did Bonnie tell you anything before she died?"

Laura looked at her oddly, and said, "No, why? What are you keeping from me?"

Mia said out loud, "Tell her something else." Bonnie thought for a minute, and spoke in Laura's ear.

"Tell her those two weeks before I passed away, she was at the hospital, and she promised me something."

Laura reported this, and Mia replied. "Any of this could have been said before she died."

Bonnie then said, "Tell her about the abortion."

Laura said out loud, "What abortion?"

Mia burst out crying. "Ok, I believe you." Mia stood up, and then sat down. She stood up again. She turned round on the spot, looking everywhere around the room. Laura stood up and held her.

"Let's just hold each other, sis, and get used to the idea: together, we're both scared, but we have each other. Remember what mom told us?"

Mia was shaking and stumbled her words as she spoke.

"Why is she still here? Why hasn't she passed on? What does she want?" All the questions came pouring out of Mia's mouth, so fast that she started to cough.

Bonnie said out loud "fetch a pen and paper"

"Quick Mia go and get a pen and paper" Laura squeaked.

Once settled Laura gazed up to the ceiling and said "ok we are listening"

Laura heard Bonnie laugh "I'm not up there you moose"

Bonnie thought of the questions that Mia had just asked her."

"Tell Mia I don't know the answer to any of her questions. I haven't actually been anywhere. I feel warm all over. I have no pain, I feel anger, frustration, and I'm tingling all over. I feel that until my anger subsides, I'm stuck on this side, but I can't help the feeling. I felt myself being pulled through a tube covered in light, like a million rainbows with colours I can't describe. It was amazing! I was spinning, turning, and having wonderful visions, which were indescribable. I could hear the smooth sound of wings in flight. Everywhere was gleaming and sparkling. It felt like it went on for a long time, but when it stopped, I was still here looking down on everyone. I never met anybody, but I know I will when my anger ebbs away – but I don't know how I know. When I looked at myself, I was glowing. I feel my body, but I know it's not solid – yet apart from tingling I can't feel it either. It's barely believable."

Laura asked Bonnie to stop for a moment while she gathered her thoughts, her hands were sweating and she was shaking all over, Mia was very pale, she looked up from reading what Laura had wrote and their eyes met, they gave each other a quivering smile. Laura sat back down and asked Bonnie to continue.

   "I also know it's wonderful here, but I'm yet to arrive. It's the weirdest feeling that I have ever felt. I can't say how I know that it's wonderful – I just do."

   Bonnie said to Laura, "I don't know why you can hear me and Mia can't, but we can get by, and hopefully you'll both hear me soon."
   Laura looked at Mia and asked her, "What's

this about an abortion, Mia?"

Mia was still crying, and Laura put her arms around her. Mia told her about last year, when she found out, she was pregnant from a one-night stand. She had become drunk and did not remember much about it. She awoke the next day to a man whom she did not know. Although she recalled dancing with everyone, she had confided in Bonnie because Bonnie knew through her work where she could get help. She worked at a youth centre, which dealt with many unwanted pregnancies.

She had also managed to secure a job there for Mia before her cancer had been diagnosed. They also dealt with many teenage pregnancies at the clinic, so Bonnie had given the contact details to Mia.

"Don't worry Mia, I understand. I'm not bothered you didn't tell me. Don't cry – it's all water under the bridge now. Let's concentrate on what Bonnie wants, and maybe we can help her get some closure."

"Thank you, Laura," Mia cried.

Mia had been ashamed: she did not want Laura to know about the abortion because Laura had tried for a family, as soon as she got married to James. Nothing had happened, though.

Mia thought to herself that perhaps it was better that James was not there: he would have carted them both off to the asylum, and they would be in strait-jackets. She smiled to herself.

Bonnie watched from the side, wishing she could be there. She put her hand on Mia's shoulder, and Mia shivered. "Oh my God, I just had a weird feeling come over me."

"What!" Laura said. "What do you mean?"

"It's as though something touched me."

Bonnie put her hand on Laura, and nothing happened. Bonnie said aloud, "I touched her, and I just touched you and nothing happened. You can hear me, Laura, but Mia can feel me. Oh, my goodness, this is wicked – she actually felt me!"

Laura repeated to Mia excitedly what Bonnie

had said. Mia sat down with her hand over her mouth in shock. Laura looked bewildered, and spoke aloud.

"Bonnie, how come I felt you blowing on me then, but not when you touched me?"

"I don't know the answers, Laura, I really don't, but that was a breath and not touch."

"Touch me again, Bonnie," Mia said excitedly.

Bonnie moved behind Mia and placed her hands on Mia's shoulders. Mia felt it immediately, and stopped herself from jumping up. She sat down and slowly took a breath. She could actually feel the hands on her shoulders.

Mia said slowly.

"This is awesome. I can feel you, Bonnie, I really can, and it feels like nothing I have felt before – it feels beautiful and peaceful."

"Good," Bonnie replied, and Laura repeated what Bonnie said. "Right," said Bonnie. "Let's talk. I want to know about Sam and who will be having him."

Laura said out loud, "He'll be staying with me. Bonnie and Mia will be coming every day to see him."

"Actually, Laura ..." Mia jumped in.

"I was going to ask you something." Laura looked at Mia, wondering *why is she acting as though I'm unapproachable?*

Mia smiled. "Laura, can I move in, and we can both take full responsibility for Sam."

Laura jumped up and swung Mia around. "Of course, of course! Why didn't I think of that? It would be ideal. I have the spare room. I can take out the desk and the old computer. I've got a laptop now, and I never go in there anyway."

"Will it be ok with James, though?"

"James is hardly here," Laura said. "We've got four bedrooms, so why would he mind, and if he does it's tough."

"Brilliant," said Mia. "I have two weeks left at the flat before my contract is up, that's why I asked now. When Mr Thomas popped round last month he mentioned it then, so I'll let him know I'll be leaving at the end of the month."

Laura felt reassured: she actually felt a black cloud lift inside her. She was sad her sister had passed away, but how many people actually got to speak to a dead sister? Not only that, but Mia was moving in with her. She realised she had been unhappy for a long time, years before they had lost Bonnie.

Bonnie started to feel warm, and spoke to Laura. "I'm glad Mia is moving in." Laura jumped again. She couldn't get used to this voice. Mia asked her why she kept jumping. Laura replied, "Because Bonnie keeps speaking to me."

Mia could only reply with a laugh. Laura said, "Come here: sit down and tell us more, Bonnie."

"I'm already sitting, you daft bats. Go and get your laptop, Laura, so you can type as I speak, it will save your hand dropping off from writing, and then Mia can read as I talk"

Laura fetched her laptop. She sat down next to Mia.

"I'm ready," Laura mumbled.

Bonnie made a weird noise. "Grrrr humph."

"What was that? Bonnie, are you still there?" Laura stood up, and Bonnie replied.

"It's ok, you just sat on me!" Bonnie started laughing out loud at Laura's face, and said, "I'm only joking, you silly cow. Sit down, and let's begin."

Mia put her hand up and exclaimed, "Wait a minute. What went on there?"

Laura disclosed what had happened and Mia said, laughing, "Don't keep things from me. It's just like Bonnie to do something like that."

Bonnie stood behind Laura and started speaking. She told the girls more about how she had felt when she passed away, how she became as light as a feather, as she emerged from her body, how she fought to remain inside herself and how angry she was for going so quickly. She explained that she felt a little better now that she could tell them what she wanted. She was going to visit Sam's father, who she had had a brief relationship with, which had ended quickly once the pregnancy was diagnosed.

Laura said out loud, "Why do you want him to know? He may want to take Sam away from us, and get parental control."

"That will never happen," said Bonnie. "I'm going to be around long enough to be certain. I'm not sure whether he'll be able to hear me. I'd like to think that as Sam gets older, he has another parent he can turn to.

"I never really gave him a chance. I ran away and never left a forwarding address. I never gave him a chance to get over the shock of the pregnancy, so I'll try and speak to him. If not, I'll have to try and learn to pick up a pen and write down my wishes."

Laura said, "Don't worry, Bonnie, you do what you have to; we'll go with whatever you want. I'm just so happy that we've got this time with you."

Bonnie realized that she only had to think of something or someone, and she would be transported to that place or near to that person. On Tuesday, she thought of Sam and found herself in his classroom. She stayed well back – she didn't want Sam to spot her. He was playing with a puzzle with another boy, and every now and then, he would giggle and point things out to his friend. Bonnie was happy. She was worried about him starting nursery, and it had put her mind at ease that he seemed settled.

Bonnie had heard Sam talking to Laura about her the previous night when she put him to bed. She was shocked when she heard him tell Laura that his mum was still around. Laura had said to him, "Let's say a prayer for your mummy," and Sam had replied.

"What for?"

Laura told him they should pray that she was happy in heaven, and Sam said.

"There is no need because my mum isn't in heaven yet!"

"What do you mean, Sam?"

"I have seen mummy a few times, and she sat

on the end of my bed."

Sam told her he had seen her trying to pick apples. Laura did not know how to respond, so she said. "Oh well, let's hope, she gets to heaven soon."

She kissed him goodnight and went down to speak to Mia about what he had said. They discussed the problem. "Well, we can't discount what he says, because we're hearing and feeling her, and now Sam is seeing her."

The following day Sam was his normal happy self, and did not mention anything else to his aunties. He didn't know if he should have told Auntie Laura about seeing his mummy. He hoped he could see her again. She looked beautiful and shiny. He knew she was an angel watching over him. He felt happy, and went to nursery singing "the wheels on the bus ..." while holding tight to his auntie's hand.

CHAPTER 4

Early, the next morning Bonnie went to visit
Max, Sam's father. She had fond memories of
her time spent with Max and regretted deeply
that she had left him, but nothing could be done
about it now. She hoped he would be able to
hear her when she found him. Bonnie started
thinking of him and visualized his face. In what
seemed like only a few seconds, she found
herself standing by a large stack of bricks. As
she turned, she saw him and caught her breath.
He was working on a construction site. He had
no top on, and his muscles were bulging on his
tanned torso. Bonnie thought he looked super-
sexy. She remembered how he had wooed her,
spending so many evenings cooking up
different pasta meals for her. He loved cooking,
and trying out different recipes. She thought
they would be together for a very long time, if
not forever. Seeing him now brought back all
the good memories of him. When she had told
him, she was pregnant, he had gone into shock.
He said he wasn't ready to become a father, and
he would rather she have a termination. Bonnie

took it badly and told him she would, but she ended the relationship, and packed up and left the area within two months. She had never seen him since. She changed her mobile phone and threw the old one in the canal – which she later regretted when her cancer was diagnosed.

They had only been together a few months, so she didn't know him well, but she was in the process of finding out where he was working when she went into the hospice. He worked at sites all over the country, so could have been anywhere.

Bonnie watched him for a while. When he was just standing without any tools or dangerous items, she slid over to him and whispered.

"Max" in his ear.

There was no response. Bonnie sighed, and her spirit sagged. She sat down on a rock watching him work Max stopped working after a while and went to sit on the rock next to where Bonnie was sitting. He opened a drink canister and took a mouthful. With a determination from within, she tried again whispering in his ear.

Max looked stunned and looked around him. There was no one around at the time. He was just having a two-minute break. He climbed across a boulder and sat on a pile of bricks, still looking around him. Bonnie knew he had heard her, so she spoke his name again. He jumped up and spun around. His face drained of colour. He spoke out loud:

"Who's there?"

"It's Bonnie."

"Where are you?" Max replied, thinking he was going mad.

Bonnie said. "You can't see me – I'm dead."

Max jumped up and darted in different directions, and finally just sat down on the ground, holding his head. Bonnie went silent for a moment, to allow him to gather his thoughts. Eventually Max looked around him and said, "Are you still there?"

Bonnie replied, "Yes."

Max was stunned and unsure whether he was hearing things or not – or maybe having a breakdown. He thought perhaps he should go to the doctor's.

"Look Max," said Bonnie, "I'm not trying to scare you. I just want you to be part of my son's life. I died of cancer three weeks ago, and I haven't yet passed to where I should be. I know I will when I'm ready, but I can't explain anything, and it drives me mad. I need to know that there will be people in my son's life, to look after him."

Max was staring at nothing. He couldn't believe what he was hearing. He must be going mad. He would have to go to the doctor's. He thought things weren't right in the head with him. He even stirred his spoon in the sugar bowl this morning when making his coffee. "I must have a brain tumour or something else seriously wrong with me. What was it, they called that disorder when you heard voices?" He tried to rack his brains to remember.

"I think I need to go and visit mom and dad, see if they're ok, and get away from this godforsaken place ... voices, can you believe it. I'm hearing voices," he said to himself.

Bonnie whispered quietly in his ear, "It's true, Max, and I'm so sorry to do this to you."

Max put his face in his hands. "That's it, I'm going. I'm not listening." He put his fingers in his ears and started walking. If this was true, not only had the love of his life died, but she had also had his son. The blood drained from his face, and he felt quite faint. He walked faster.

Bonnie rushed after him. She was calling him, but with fingers stuck in his ears she was not getting through. Bonnie rushed in front of him and put her hands up. He came to a standstill. Max fell to the floor, covered in dust and on his knees, he started to vomit. It was slowly occurring to him that what was happening was real.

He thought when Bonnie left him that it was because he'd wanted her to have an abortion, and that once she had terminated the pregnancy she could not bear to be near him. For God's sake, he saw her two months after that, shopping in town: she hadn't looked pregnant, and it took all his might not to run over to her begging for forgiveness.

He spoke very quietly, saying, "What is his name, Bonnie?"

Bonnie watched him. She could tell he was devastated by her death. She could feel it inside herself, and she felt guilty for running away.

"His name is Sam," she said.

"And how old is he?"

Bonnie went silent, and Max said, "I know he's four, and his birthday is in March."

"How did you know that, then?" replied Bonnie.

Max whispered, "Because that's what I calculated a long time ago. I kept thinking if you'd had the baby, then that's how old he would be. I never thought for a minute that you would go ahead with the pregnancy. I was so devastated when you left. I wanted to say sorry ... that I never meant what I said. I would have got over the shock, and we could have had the baby. I'm so sorry, Bonnie, I really am."

"What's done is done, Max," Bonnie replied. "Can we talk somewhere so we can make arrangements for Sam?"

"Sure," said Max. "I'll take the rest of the day off work and tell my manager I'm feeling dizzy." It wasn't far from the truth. Max had tears trickling down his cheeks. Bonnie wiped them away with the tip of her finger, and he jumped back with a jolt.

"What was that? My God, something touched me!"

"It's ok, Max, it was me. I'm sorry, I won't do it again." Max was turning on the spot, and finding it hard to stand. His manager saw him from the cabin window and shouted.

"Max, do you want me to call someone?"

"No, Chris, I need to go home I'm feeling quite ill.

"You carry on son you look awful" his gaffer shouted.

"I'll ring you tomorrow if I can't come in." Max shouted.

Chris watched him leave. He thought Max looked unwell, pale, and weak. He hoped his condition was nothing serious.

Bonnie asked him again if there was anywhere quiet, they could go to talk. Max looked around again for her. He was in complete disbelief.

"You knocked me over earlier didn't you?"

"Yes it was me, I needed you to stop and listen."

"We can go to the park and walk around; it's peaceful during the day while the kids are at school."

Bonnie felt her heart flip at his words. She knew that although her heart was not actually there, she still had all her feelings – especially the anger: it kept reeling up and swallowing her. She couldn't pinpoint the problem, but she was feeling slightly better about Sam's future now and a slight sense of ease was flowing through her, however, underneath, the anger was still rumbling.

She followed behind Max as he walked towards the park. The large iron gates looming before them were over a hundred years old, and although the park was refurbished, they maintained that solid, impregnable Victorian look. She felt glad that she wasn't so solid and heavy, grateful for her freedom of movement.

Max sat under a weeping willow, next to the brook: he didn't want to look like an unhinged person if anyone noticed him talking to himself. There was a small stream with a watery carpet of pebbles and stones. A gentle current of water rolled over them with the slightest tinkling sound.

It was very peaceful here in the spring. Later, it would be noisier. In the summer months, families came with picnics and the children splashed in the water. The more adventurous ones tried jumping the brook. Further down the stream was wider and a thick rope had been fixed to a branch, so the older children took turns to swing over to the other side.

Max was immersed in his own thoughts when he suddenly remembered why he was here. He still did not know if he was imagining Bonnie so he whispered her name. She answered immediately, "I'm here, Max."

"Ok," Max said. "What do you want me to do?"

"I need you to visit Sam at my house and very slowly get to know him, spending a few hours a week. Later you could maybe take him out a few times, and eventually I'd like you to have him each weekend." Max was looking worried. Bonnie noticed.

"It might take twelve months or more. Max, I want him to love you, and get to know you really well."

Max thought there was nothing he'd like more.

"What about Sam? How will I explain to him that I'm his father?"

"Don't worry: Sam has seen me, and I am keeping out of his way so as not to confuse him." Bonnie told Max that he could tell Sam that his mom had sent him.

"I want him to get to know his daddy." Max put his hands over his face and began to weep. He couldn't stop. The tears came fast, an endless rivulet. Bonnie put her hands on his shoulders. He jumped up, and Bonnie exclaimed, "You felt me! Max, you felt me!"

"Yes, I did, just like earlier... oh, my God. What's going on? I'm going mad."

"No, you're not, Max. Some people can hear me, and some can feel me. It's the same with my sisters. You're lucky you can do both."

"You mean you've been speaking to other people?"

"Yes," said Bonnie. "I've got my two sisters. Mia can feel me and Laura can hear me. I'll let them know you'll be contacting them, and later coming round – and by the way, I want you to remember that Sam is to always to stay at Laura's. She'll be his main carer, along with Mia. I don't want the chain broken." Max was willing to agree to anything to see his son.

"Ok, Bonnie, I hear you. I'll do what you say. When do you want me to visit?"

"As soon as possible. You'll need to ring them. I want to watch what happens, so it must be before I have to go."

"When do you have to go?"

"I'm not sure. I know I'll get the feeling but I don't know when. There's so much I don't understand but so much more that I do ... I can't explain things at this moment ... I'm very confused."

Max asked Bonnie for Laura's phone number and she gave it him, adding, "Don't ring for a few days. I need to speak to them both, and then you can arrange to meet at the house."

Bonnie said goodbye to Max and told him she would speak to him again soon.

Bonnie floated off down the street, a little more at ease but angry that she had never tried to contact Max after Sam had been born ... angry that she had let Max go without thinking it through.

She watched Max walk off and felt sad that she had misread the situation ... but she knew she couldn't turn back time ... so she just watched him walk away.

She suddenly heard her name called. It felt like it came from behind her. Then she heard it again. She turned, and there was no one there. She heard her name a third time and asked, "Who is this? Who can see me?"

"My name is Robert," said a man's voice. As she turned, he was standing directly behind her. She stared at him, but did not recognise him. There was a shine to his appearance, which was somehow very peaceful. His hair was brushed back, and his eyes were striking. He towered over her: she thought he must be at least six feet tall.

"I've been sent to speak to you." Bonnie grinned at him. "What do you mean, you've been sent?"

"I've come to guide you, Bonnie." She wondered if she could take this man seriously.

"I don't want guiding, thanks. I'm ok. I'm sorting out my life." Rob sighed, and Bonnie glared at him.

"That's not how it happens, my dear," he replied. "I need to help you let go of your anger, and you need to come with me." Bonnie could feel herself getting angrier.

"I'm not going anywhere, thanks. I'm happy where I am, so you can go back to where you came from, ok? I can't go anywhere yet – I have so much to do."

Robert replied, "My dear, I need you to come with me." Bonnie felt scared; she felt a strong pull towards this man ... she felt drawn towards him despite herself, as if she didn't have a choice.

"Please ... I need to arrange things. I can't go anywhere." Robert didn't want her to be scared.

"We realised that and gave you some time, but your anger is holding you back. You're full of rage." Bonnie started weeping. Real tears were falling. "How is this?" she thought.

"Can I ask you something, Rob?"

"Yes of course, you can ask me anything, and I'll tell you as much as you want to know."

"Why didn't I cross over? I saw the most amazing light, and then I was back here floating around."

Robert looked at her with a gleam in his eye. "Yes, this is normal. If you'd gone towards the light you would never have wanted to come back, but it was your anger that held you back."

Bonnie was a little confused.

"So what's behind the light?"

"Behind the light is a magic you'll have to wait to see. I can't explain how beautiful it is, but everything will become clear when you get there."

Bonnie smiled. He seemed to have calmed her. "So can I have a peek before I go?"

"No, not yet my dear. First, tell me how I can help you to shed your anger. I'll be with you until you go and I'll be by your side, but it's best not to tell your sisters I'm here."

"Well, I think most of my fury is from having to leave Sam. He's so young, and I love him so much – it's not fair. I won't be able see him grow up."

Rob pondered what Bonnie had said, then gently laid a hand on her shoulder.

"The thing is, my dear, you'll see him grow up. You can be by his side for as long as you want."

"Well, how come you've come to get me, then?" Bonnie replied.

"It's different; you're still allowed to visit once you've reached your realm. I never said I had come to get you. I said I needed you to come with me."

"What do you mean my realm?" Bonnie squeaked.

"Well, it's peaceful, beautiful, and calm, and it's yours. You always have a window, so you can always see out. Now you're stuck, as we put it, and you need help to release your anger. No one reaches their own special place until they're free of bad feeling. It normally happens on your journey to us, but for some reason you were still full of resentment, so you missed the boat so to speak."

"Hell, Rob!"

"I think you should find a better turn of phrase, my dear. Certain people wouldn't appreciate that kind of language."

"Oh sorry ... well, God almighty."

"Ahem"

"Oh, shit ... sorry, that's bad too ... I don't know what to say."

"How about, 'Well, I say.' That might be better," said Rob.

"Well, I say," said Bonnie, laughing. "Well, I say. I think 'Oh shit' sounds better though, don't you?"

Bonnie tittered. Rob chuckled.

"You've got a lot to learn, my dear."

Bonnie thought of Laura, and immediately found herself in Laura's house. Rob was beside her. She floated right up behind Laura, and shouted "Boo!" Laura jumped and spun round, shouting. "Stop it! Just stop making me jump! It's not funny – my heart's racing. You'll give me a heart attack, and I'll end up next to you, you fool!"

"Sorry," said Bonnie. "I was excited. I do have something to tell you – guess what? I've met someone." Bonnie started laughing. Laura looked bemused.

"Who have you met? Tell me."

"He's from heaven, and he's staying with me until I go to the other side." Rob laughed too.

"I told you not to tell them." But he was still laughing at Bonne's excitement.

Mia had moved into Laura's spare room. She was happy to be living with Laura and Sam. Just being close to, Laura at this time was enough, but having Sam was a bonus ... and when Sam got too demanding she could help by taking him out for a few hours. It would work out well; as Mia worked mornings, she'd be able to collect Sam from nursery.

CHAPTER 5

Mia worked at the teenagers' centre in Bromsgrove just a few miles from them; she dealt with all sorts of teenage problems, including pregnancy and runaways. Bonnie had got her the job just after she was diagnosed. She knew Mia would love it. Mia only worked until one o'clock, so she'd be back at Laura's in time to pick Sam up. They both wanted him to feel secure, and would only use babysitters as a last resort. She had booked the next day off ready for the visitor.

Tomorrow morning Max was coming round to meet the girls. He had phoned the evening before and told them who he was. He said that Bonnie had told him they would be expecting him. Laura had laughed and said, "Yes, I know."

Max was shaking all over when he put the phone down. He didn't know whether to visit his doctor or a priest – either would be embarrassing. The doctor might just cart him off to an asylum if he said what was going on.

He was sure there was a name for hearing voices in your head, and it felt weird that he had just spoken to a woman he had never met ... and she was expecting him.

Max was unsure how he was going to feel when he saw Sam for the first time. He had spent the last few nights so upset. He couldn't stop the tears when he thought of Bonnie: he ached so badly, full of regret for what he had done to her, and he berated himself for not chasing her and finding where she had gone. He knew he couldn't have stopped her illness, but the thought of not being there for her and their son caused him intense pain.

Max woke early the next day, showered, and got himself ready early. He paced the floor for an hour and a half until he knew it was time to leave.

Laura and Mia were both sitting down, drinking coffee and discussing Max, when the doorbell rang. They both jumped. Then Bonnie said, "Come on Laura, he's here." Laura jumped again. She couldn't get used to hearing Bonnie's voice.

Mia opened the door to see a lovely-looking man, but he was shaking all over. She pulled him in and said, "Coffee, mate? We're in the same boat, remember. No need to have kittens on the doorstep. I won't eat you – though you do look very tasty." She then flew backwards and landed on the stairs. Bonnie had given her a shove, and was laughing.

"Why is Bonnie laughing?" said Laura. Mia started laughing.

"She just pushed me over for saying I wanted to eat Max," Laura laughed. She put the kettle on. She'd thought, like Mia, that this man was gorgeous: his eyes were amazing – you could dive right into them. Max just had an amazed look on his face.

"I take it you're not used to having Bonnie around as much as we are," Mia said. Rob just shook his head in bewilderment.

"Come and sit down, Max. We're as nervous as you."

Max sat down. He liked Bonnie's sisters immediately, on sight, and knew he was going to get on well with them. He looked at Laura and she reminded him of Bonnie. His heart skipped a beat. She was beautiful – very similar to Bonnie – but with longer hair and a cute nose. He took a deep breath and told them about his job, and where he was living. They spoke about Sam and how they would introduce him to Max. Bonnie whispered in Laura's ear, as quietly as she could.

 "Go and get a pen and paper.

" Laura just flinched, but said out loud, "That's so much better, Bonnie. Please speak like that in future."

 Max looked at Laura and said, "I heard her whisper, too."

   Mia just looked upset. She couldn't believe she was the only one who couldn't hear anything.

   Bonnie mentioned some things to Laura that she wanted to happen, and told her to write them down so that Mia would be in the picture – they could refer to these plans later. Bonnie wanted Sam to meet Max, but not to be told immediately that he was his daddy. She wanted him to get to know and love him slowly. They all agreed that this was a brilliant strategy.

"Are you going to stay today for tea, and meet Sam when I fetch him from school?" Mia said to Max.

"If you don't mind – I'd like that," Max said.

At a quarter to three, Mia drove to the school and collected Sam. She told him they had a visitor: an old friend of his mom. Sam said he didn't remember, and Mia told him she had known this man before Sam was born. That suited him fine, and he skipped along holding Mia's hand.

Once in the house, Sam went straight up to Max and said, "Hello." Max returned the greeting and asked to be excused, asking where the bathroom was. Once there he covered his face with his hands and sobbed so hard he thought, he would collapse. Laura came up the stairs, leaving Mia to make a sandwich for Sam. She knocked gently on the bathroom door.

"Let me in, Max love – come on, we're all

feeling the same."

Max opened the door. He was feeling embarrassed about his behaviour. Laura put her arms around him. She felt sad for him. It felt so right holding him: it was a feeling she hadn't experienced for too long. She could feel his taut muscles, and it gave her an urge to caress him. It made her realise that she had no feelings for James at all. This stranger had made her aware of that. She held him for a long time while he cried.

When Max had calmed down, he said.

I'm ready to spend some time with Sam now."

. Laura made him a coffee first, and told him to take ten minutes to become calmer. When he was ready, Max went into the living room and sat playing with Sam and his cars. Father and son were already starting to get on very well. Bonnie was watching this special moment, but she kept silent and just observed the proceedings. She felt free inside herself for the first time since she had passed away.

Laura was watching them closely too. She'd

been feeling down over the last few days. James hadn't contacted her since the funeral. It seemed to her that they were growing further apart all the time. James had told her he was fine with Sam and Mia being there. There were no phones calls or texts to make her worry about her marriage. She had tried to ring him more than once, and either he hadn't been there or had spoken very briefly, saying he was busy. It never used to be like this, she thought, and she felt a sense of impending doom. She shook herself and came back to the present. It looked like Sam and Max were getting on famously.

"Auntie Lar, look quick! Max has made me a garage. I haven't got a garage, look!"

Max had used the cardboard box that Sam's cars had come in. He had made a fantastic garage for him, using his creative imagination.

"Wow, what a brilliant garage," Laura said. She looked at Max and gave him a wink. He hadn't turned his head away from Sam for an hour. Max couldn't take his eyes off him – he knew he loved him already; he knew he would die for this little boy if he had to.

Bonnie felt the bond too, and experienced an overpowering rush of love for both of them. She knew she was losing her anger: she could feel her soul getting lighter all the time. A powerful thought came to her when she saw Max look at Laura for the first time: this might just work ... she could sort this.

Laura was upstairs in the bathroom when she heard Bonnie whisper – it was so much better than being made to jump out of one's skin every other minute of the day.

Laura laughed and said aloud, "I don't need to change my knickers any more, Bonnie."

Bonnie laughed, too. She didn't realise she'd been so alarming. Laura turned and looked out of the window.

"I'll never be scared about dying now I've heard you, Bonnie."

Bonnie said she was glad about that.

"Bonnie."

"Yes, Laura?"

"Do you think Max is handsome?"

"Well, yes, I suppose he is," Laura replied. "Why?"

"I just wondered," said Bonnie.

"Hey, I hope you're not thinking what I'm thinking! I'm married, Bonnie." Laura heard Bonnie giggle, and she said, "I wish I could see your cheeky face again, Bonnie. I'm sure I know what face you're pulling now, you minx!"

Laura went quiet for a while, then asked her sister, "Have you seen mom?"

"No the only person I have met is Rob, but I know mum is close.

She tried to explain the feeling that she had most of the time: she was close to the other side, but couldn't actually pass through until she was ready. Rob had told her more, explaining details, and she was more understanding of the situation. She'd been angry before, so she couldn't think clearly.

CHAPTER 6

Laura had received some mail that morning, but had left it on a pile in the hallway. When she eventually opened it, she found a solicitor's letter from James. She had put it out of her mind. All her feelings were jumbled up at the moment. Laura couldn't stop thinking about Max now, and it was all Bonnie's fault. She kept watching him when he was around, and he had caught her a few times. Once he asked if he had any food left on his face from dinner, and then she had gone red, which made it worse. If Bonnie had not already been dead, she could have murdered her.

Mia was happy. She liked Max, and understood what Bonnie had seen in him. She knew he would make a perfect father for Sam. She also loved her job. She had moved into Laura's home and she was happy for the first time since Bonnie died – but she was worried for Laura. Laura had not heard from James, and she knew it was on her mind. She had been very quiet this morning, but wouldn't say why.

Mia knew something was happening but did not know what; she would try and speak to her later.

The next morning Max came and took Sam to school. He'd taken a week off work to spend as much time with Sam as possible. Sam loved him already, so he was happy when the doorbell rang.

"Bye Auntie Lar, bye Auntie Mia, see you later."

"Bye Sam, see you later, be good." They both kissed him and came back into the kitchen. Max was coming back for coffee after dropping Sam at school. Mia said, immediately after the door shut, "What's going on, Laura? You're shutting me out, and I know something's going on." Laura looked at Mia and told her she had received a letter from a solicitor that James had contacted her through, he wanted a divorce. He had found someone else, and was never coming back from Europe. Mia went over and put her arms around Laura.

"Don't worry: I'm glad, because she I'm not in love with James anymore."

She had realised it after Bonnie died. He had given her no support at all, and it proved how he really felt. All she felt was total relief. She felt betrayed because of him seeing someone else, but to be fair she had not thought of him much at all. James must have been worried though, because he had offered her the house, fully paid off by him, and a £50,000-pound settlement, for a quick divorce.

Mia's mouth was wide open: she was so shocked she couldn't speak. "Close your mouth, love," said Laura, laughing.

"How can you laugh?" Laura just looked at her with a gleam in her eyes, and pressed "Play" on the cd player. She grabbed Mia and started swinging her round the kitchen, laughing.

"I'm so happy, Mia. I was going to give him a few months, and if he hadn't contacted me or tried to get home for a weekend I was going to end the marriage anyway. Now he's sorted it all out for me, he can have his quickie divorce and I'll find a job. There's no rush. I have fifty grand to see me through the next few years.

*** *** ***

Rob was close to Bonnie, and Bonnie felt him – she spoke to him all the time. He gave her answers and helped her so much with her unending questions.

Rob spoke and explained that her son was going to be very happy, and that he was safe. It was time to deal with another reason for Bonnie's anger.

Bonnie could not think of anything that she was angry about, other than dying too early and leaving Sam behind.

Rob told her to think back to when she was alive, and when she was angry. Bonnie said it was her mom dying, but that anyone would feel the same.

Rob said, "Come on, Bonnie, we're going on a journey." He held her hand, and she could see light. She knew where she was going and screamed for Rob to let her go. He said he couldn't, but promised he would bring her back immediately after the visit. Bonnie calmed down: the thought of not being able to speak to

Laura or watch Sam horrified her, but Rob was going to explain things. He thought it would be best for her to see for herself a glimpse of what was to come: and that was when Bonnie's eyes were really opened for the first time.

CHAPTER 7

"The light"

Everywhere she looked; it was just lights and love. It was so hard for her to explain. The lights were blinding but magnificent, and the colours were amazing – so bright. All the colours mixed into one beautiful prism. The overall sensation was of total euphoria. She felt an immediate attachment.

"Rob, where are we?"

"We're on the way to meet your mother."

Bonnie was flabbergasted. Her heart felt as though it was beating very quickly, even though she knew she didn't have one. It was an amazing sensation. She had the impression that she was flying: she felt no wind in her hair, but she could see different images as she travelled. There were fields of poppies and high mountains ... she felt thrilled, and full up with emotion. She put her hands up to her face and felt real tears.

"Why's that, Rob? I've got real tears."

"That's quite common when your emotions are strong. You're still dead, if that's what you're wondering about." Rob smiled at her, and she laughed at his face. All too soon, she was standing on her feet, looking down onto a beach. She stared into the distance and noticed a figure. From the tip of her toes to her head, she felt as though she was on fire: her emotions were so strong. She stood stock-still for a moment, and then started to run.

Mary was standing on the beach holding a small baby about four months old. She saw Bonnie and put the baby down. Bonnie was running towards her. As Mary turned and saw Bonnie she opened her arms wide, and Bonnie flew into them. It was miraculous: it was as if she was still alive. She felt as though she was whole. As she held her mother, she was so happy. Mary looked at Bonnie with such intense love that it seemed to soak through her and fill her up. She was astounded to find that she was actually holding her wonderful mother in her arms.

"Mum I love you so much."

Mary replied, "I love you too darling, when you pass over properly I'll be here waiting for you and I'll bring Nan and granddad too, so don't be worried."

"Worried?" said Bonnie. "I don't want to go back now!" She was soaked with love, and did not want to lose it.

"Who does the baby belong to?"

"It's Mia's baby."

Bonnie picked up the little girl and cooed at her. "She is beautiful."

She had a little button nose and deep blue eyes; her hair was curly and dark. Bonnie started asking questions, but Rob stopped her and told her he would explain later.

Mary told Bonnie she wanted her to pass the message on to her girls that she loved them dearly; she had visited on a few occasions; she had also attended Sam's birth.

"You need to speak to the girls for me Bonnie,

tell them I love them." Mary sounded desperate.

"I will mum I promise."

Bonnie and Mary walked and chatted for a while. "Is this feeling always with you?" she asked her mother.

Mary asked her if she meant the feeling of love.

"Yes," Bonnie replied. Mary looked at her with a smile and said, "Yes, you always feel it, and you're very lucky to be able to sample it."

Holding hands, they walked along the beach. Bonnie's eyes were wide open like that of scared rabbit. She did not want to blink in case she missed anything, even the smallest detail she wanted to catch, like a camcorder, so she could rewind later.

The beach was magical. The sea was real. It was tranquil but there was a tiny breeze, not enough to move your hair but noticeable nonetheless.

Mary explained to her, "You get what you really want on this side. I always wanted to be on a beautiful beach when I was alive, and now I spend lots of my time here. I love it."

Rob was touching Bonnie's shoulder. He said, "Come on, Bonnie – we must get back."

Bonnie really felt like staying little longer.

"This will still be here when you return, but you have unfinished business to attend to."

With a flash, Bonnie realised that she was back on the earth plane, and was walking, holding Rob's arm. She asked him about the baby, and he told her that all babies who are lost, whether by miscarriage or abortion, carry on into the afterlife.

"They are looked after by relatives, and grow over there until it's time to meet their birth mothers again."

Bonnie didn't understand how the mothers would recognise them. Rob told her that they automatically recognise their children when they pass over.

"We don't have the same time scale that you do on the earthly plain, that's why you don't have time to be in both, my dear. When you pass through, you'll have the answer to every question you have ever asked – I promise you everything will become clear."

As Rob and Bonnie walked, she told him about the great relationship all the girls had with their mum.

"I wish Laura and Mia could have met mum. I think Laura would recover properly from mum's death if she could only experience what I have a moment ago.

"It is "almost impossible."

Bonnie jumped up and grabbed Rob by the arm, saying, "What do you mean, 'almost'? Tell me, Rob, if there's any chance whatsoever that my sisters can experience that, then I want it to happen."

Rob turned to Bonnie and explained.

"Everything that happens has to be for the higher good of that person. It is hard for me to explain how things work: I have only shown you love, but there is "so much more that you will understand when you pass over."

Rob told her he would look into it, which made Bonnie happy, for the moment – but she knew it was out of the question for this to happen now: she just had to bide her time.

*** *** ***

Mia was feeling happy, considering her family losses – first her mom, and now her sister – but she knew now that there was an afterlife, and it warmed her. She had also taken more hours on at work recently because Max was playing such a big part in Sam's life, collecting him from school most days.

She had recently met a man she liked at work. He had worked in her department for more than six years, and had known Bonnie well before she became ill. Mia had not met him until last week, and had gone weak at the knees when he spoke to her. She vaguely remembered him from Bonnie's funeral, but was not in any state to notice anything at the time. She was feeling very young again. He had asked her out for a meal, and she had arranged to go with him to an Italian restaurant in town on Friday night. She knew Laura was staying in because Max was coming round for tea after taking Sam to the cinema, so she was excited and looking forward to the meal. Laura smiled when she told her; "Brian is a lovely person I'm glad for you." Laura had met Brian a few times through Bonnie, and she thought he was a gentleman, "As far as I'm concerned he will do for you."

"Hold on a minute," Mia said. "It's my first date, not a marriage proposal."

Laura and Mia both stood laughing and Bonnie stood behind them both saying nothing, just watching with a warm feeling flowing through her. She knew things were going to work out well.

CHAPTER 8

The next day, Thursday, Mia was at home. It was her day off so they had planned a day together. Max was coming over to pick Sam up after nursery and he would be bringing him home later, after his trip to the park. It had only been three weeks since he had met him, and Max was all Sam talked about from morning to night. He came to the house every day, whether he picked Sam up or not, and he was enjoying the company of the girls – especially Laura, with whom he "felt a connection". He said nothing, but thought she was brilliant. She reminded him a little of Bonnie, and he loved the way she blushed if he looked at her.

Mia could see what was going on between them, but said nothing. She hoped and prayed that this would turn into something special. She wanted to speak to Bonnie about it, but she had not heard from her for the last two days. She would mention it as soon as she was on her own and knew Bonnie was there.

Mia went upstairs to give the bedrooms a good clean. No real housework had been accomplished since the funeral, so she stripped all the beds and opened the windows to let in some fresh air; she hummed as she went along, happy in herself. As she turned, she stood on a sharp toy on the floor and jumped around the room, holding her injured foot.

"Shit! Shit! Shit!"

Mia fell over and landed on the floor with a bump, which took the wind out of her. Laura came running up the stairs. After one look at Mia she started laughing uncontrollably, tears rolling down her face, holding her sides and crossing her legs.

"Damn you, Laura, it's not funny."

This made Laura laugh even more. Mia saw the funny side once the pain subsided, and they ended up giggling together. They hadn't felt this type of connection for a long while.

Bonnie was watching, and she started laughing too. Laura heard her and looked up towards the sound. Tears started falling – tears of sadness.

"I want you back, Bonnie! I miss you."

Bonnie stopped laughing. She saw Laura's anguish.

"Don't be sad, love. You know I'm here, and you know there's more when you pass over. This should put your mind at rest." Laura dropped her head into her hands.

"It's you I want, Bonnie! You, as in your whole self. "Oh god I'm just having a difficult moment. Ignore me."

Mia sat there, knowing that Bonnie was talking to Laura. She felt so frustrated that she couldn't hear her. Just then she felt two hands on her shoulders and a lovely feeling coursed through her. It was exquisite, a really weird but wonderful feeling. She had never felt before. It was like being smothered with love, a euphoria of love she could not describe.

Laura asked her what was wrong. Mia tried to explain the feeling to her.

Bonnie told Laura that she had seen and felt love like no other love that she would feel in this life, no matter how happy she was, and she had just passed a little of it on to Mia when she touched her.

Laura watched Mia's face and was envious.

"Oh Mia I would love to feel that, and you should not worry now about being unable to hear Bonnie. Just think of that feeling she gave you"

Mia agreed. "That feeling will stay with me forever, and although I can't explain it I will never forget it."

Bonnie laughed and told Laura that, as the time drew closer for her to leave, the feeling would get stronger – so if she touched Mia again it would be a stronger feeling. Laura laughed and said she didn't think Mia could take much more, "judging from the look on her face". They both laughed.

Laura went downstairs to put the kettle on.

Mia said,

"Bonnie if you're there, just touch me quickly."

She did. Mia told Bonnie about her feeling that Laura and Max were getting close. She needed to know how Bonnie felt about it. Mia asked Bonnie to try to let her know her feelings about the situation. Mia carried on with her cleaning regime, and managed to finish all the upstairs rooms in a few hours.

Laura called Mia to come down for a coffee.

"I made you two coffees that have gone cold. You need to relax for a while. The upstairs is lovely."

Mia looked around her. She leant over the banister.

"Yes, it is nice, but for how long?"

"Well, it'll be until Sam comes home, then it may look like a hurricane's passed through."

"No it won't, silly. He'll be so excited going to the cinema with Max that he'll be dressed and changed in record time, and shattered when he comes back – so we've got a respite till tomorrow afternoon." They both smiled.

Meanwhile Bonnie was outside, with Rob by

her side. She was watching people in the street: there were numerous individuals everywhere: some were shining, some looked as though beams of light were projecting through their bodies. She was watching in amazement.

"Where are all these people coming from?" she asked Rob. He told her they were "spirits like you, visiting or helping people".

"Why am I seeing them now? I'm confused."

"You're getting nearer to acceptance of your situation: your anger is leaving you and you'll see a lot more before you finally cross over."

This made her feel a bit better and also proved that she would be able to visit whenever she felt the need to, Rob told her she should not be frightened of leaving when she finally crossed over.

"Your eyes will be opened now Bonnie and you will see more spirit people."

Bonnie was feeling so deliriously warm and happy. She told Rob that she was feeling better and better as the time passed. Still, she did not want to go until she saw her family settled and happy. She told Rob what Mia had asked of her.

"Would that bother you, Bonnie?"

"No, not all. I'd love Max and Laura to get together, nothing would make me happier." She wondered to herself why she didn't feel jealous – when she had seen Max on the building site she had felt herself melt. Oh, well, she knew she would be happy.

She didn't want to tell Max and Laura that this was what they must do, but she wanted them to know she would be happy if they did get together; "Being dead does something for you," she thought to herself.

Rob told Bonnie to write a note for Mia, "short and sweet", saying it was fine for them to get together, and she wasn't to worry.

Bonnie managed to write down her thoughts. She had to concentrate so hard to pick the pen up, she left the note on Mia's pillow and went to speak to Laura. She told Laura to tell Mia to go to her room for a moment.

"Why?" Laura asked. Bonnie told her, "Trust me." Mia went upstairs. Bonnie told Laura that Max thought Laura was beautiful. Laura scoffed and said she was imagining it. A red blush crept up Laura's neck, and Bonnie laughed.

"Stop teasing me, Bonnie. This is the man you were so in love with, and had a child with." "you've no worries on that score: I'm not on the earthly plane."

Although she was very fond of Max, she explained that the only thing keeping her here was the happiness of everyone else who was close to her.

"Mia is on her way to happiness. I can see you are too, but it may take time."

"My little Sam is really happy, so that makes me happy, and the happier I become the further Rob takes me to see where my place is."

Laura felt a surge of emotions all at once. She was still legally married. She thought she was falling in love with her dead sister's ex, and she had lost her lovely sister. She told

Bonnie that she was not happy for her to leave. Bonnie explained that Rob had told her she could visit any time and that there were many spirit people walking up and down the street. She told her that she had also seen them. Laura laughed: Bonnie was still just as funny as before. Laura started to feel that things might come together, but she told Bonnie, "I do have feelings for Max, but I'll never make the first move, so don't interfere – or else."

Bonnie laughed. "Ok," she said.

**

Mia read the note and felt relieved. She didn't know how she had done it, but she had. It was Bonnie's writing, she knew: no one could copy it. Bonnic had left her notes all the time when she was alive. She still could not believe that this was happening to her. Her dead sister was still in contact with her – it amazed her. But she was delighted that Bonnie was in favour of Max and Laura getting together.

CHAPTER 9

On Friday morning, while Mia was getting ready for work, she was humming to herself.

"Why are you humming?" Sam said to his auntie, as he jumped all over his bed.

"Because I'm feeling happy, that's why," she told him. Sam said he was happy too. He had loads of new friends at nursery, and he was going to be running in the egg and spoon race next week. Mia laughed and told him he would do well. If he was as fast on the track as he was at home, she knew he would do well.

Sam told her his mom had promised to be there. Mia stopped and looked at Sam.

"When did mommy tell you that?"

"She told me last night, when I was in bed; she sits on my bed all the time. I'm sad I can't have her back, but I'm happy she's an angel and she still comes to see me. Anyway, can I have my breakfast, Auntie Mia? I'm starving!"

Mia gave his head a rub and said, "Come on then, you little toe rag – be quick. I have to get to work."

Laura was still in the bathroom, so she put Sam's Coco Pops on the table and left him to eat. She wondered why Sam could see Bonnie. It still irked her that she could only feel her, but she was glad for Sam.

Mia told Laura what Sam had told her, and Laura laughed and said they were fortunate they all had the opportunity to have Bonnie still in their lives – but she was shocked that Sam was experiencing this phenomenon.

Later, Bonnie was out walking with Rob. He told her she had a lot to learn. Some of the spirits she was seeing had prisms of light shooting from their backs. She asked Rob who these individuals were, and he told her they were angels. Bonnie was watching them. They seemed to glisten like snow crystals. They were walking close to, or beside, particular people.

"Why couldn't I see these angels before?" she said. Rob placed a hand on her shoulder. "The closer you get to your realm, the more you will see."

"The angels are around everyone – we all have them. They're close to us at all times." Bonnie crinkled her eyes up in confusion

"I promise you will understand everything very soon."

All of a sudden, she saw a man running behind a woman. Her angel was pushing against her as the man grabbed her bag and pushed her to the ground. It happened so quickly. Bonnie shouted to Rob to do something.

"You can't help, I'm afraid Bonnie: her angel has everything under control."

Another passer-by had given chase and was racing after the robber. They both disappeared out of sight. The woman had got up from the ground, but was visibly shaken. Her angel beckoned Rob and Bonnie to come over, and asked them to link their arms with his around the woman. As they did so they felt the woman relax slightly. She was taking deep breaths, and she became calmer.

"Pissing idiot!" she shouted. Bonnie and Rob laughed.

The angel gave a look that said, "I'd like to laugh too", but he didn't. The woman reached her home and started to go through her gate, still swearing. The young man who had chased the robber came running up with her bag – and a bloody nose.

"Oh My God!" the woman exclaimed. "Thank you so much. Quick, come in – let me sort out your face, it's the least I can do." They both went inside.

Bonnie was looking sad, and Rob asked her why. She told him how painful her life had been, and about all the recent events that had been so distressing. She said she wished that her life had been better. Rob stopped her and said, "There's a lot of bad, Bonnie, but a lot of things happen for a reason. Sometimes you don't know why, and you'll never find out until you die. I'll let you into a secret. That woman you just saw is sixty-eight years old, and that man who chased the robber is twenty-nine years old. The woman's name is Eileen, and she has a son she fell out with over five years ago. It just so happens that the chaser knows her son. Now she's going to chat to that man for a long while, and her angel will make magic today."

"I can't believe it," said Bonnie. Rob looked at Bonnie, tilted his head to one side, and gave her a knowing look.

"Have you ever had something happen and you say to yourself, 'I can't believe that – I was only just thinking of that person, and I've just bumped into her after so long'? Or you do something, or go somewhere, and say to yourself, 'If that hadn't happened, something else wouldn't have.' Angels are with us all the time, guiding us to make life-changing decisions. Well, that's what life is about: we all have paths to follow, and we have choices to make, and sometimes we make the wrong choices. Eileen has been feeling guilty about her son lately, and he's been on her mind. Her angel is giving her a chance." Bonnie was perplexed.

"But she could have been hurt. Couldn't it have been made simpler?"

"Not really, because Eileen isn't the type to invite strangers into her house, but this worked! There are reasons for everything that happens, and as I've said before when you finally pass over everything will become clear, my dear."

Bonnie was starting to understand. Every day she spent with Rob; more things she thought were complex became clearer.

CHAPTER 10

Mia arrived home from work. She was excited about the evening to come. She kissed Sam on her way into the kitchen and gave Laura a hug. She made herself a cup of tea. Mia seemed in a world of her own, and Laura asked her if she was anticipating her romantic meal. Mia laughed and said, "Yes, I'm *really* looking forward to it." Brian was picking her up at 7.30, so she had a few hours to get ready.

Laura gave her sister a wink.

"Now then, Mia, you can bring him back if you want."

"Don't be so cheeky. If I'm thinking what you're thinking, I'm not going to be doing anything like that."

Laura laughed.

"I meant for a coffee!" However, Mia knew exactly what she was hinting at, and pulled her tongue out as she went upstairs for a shower.

Max poked his head round the kitchen door and whispered to Laura, "Sam's fallen asleep."

"Oh, blast it, Max, he was supposed to be going to the cinema with you, but he would have fallen asleep there, I suppose."

"Well, we can go tomorrow." Max smiled, and Laura turned crimson.

"And if you want you can come too, and we'll have lunch afterwards." Laura felt the blood rush up her neck again. Max winked at her and said, "Don't worry – we've got Sam with us, so we can't sit in the back row!"

Laura's face was burning, and she cursed herself for being so open. She started coughing to cover herself. Laura could hardly look at him lately without going red. She couldn't speak ... she got tongue-tied, and she was sure he knew and was poking fun at her.

"Are you up for it then, Laura?" She nodded, and said, "Yes, that would be nice – thank you," her heart beating a million times a minute. Max smiled as he went into the living room and winked at Sam, who was pretending quite brilliantly to be asleep. Max whispered in his ear, "Thank you son," and Sam kissed him on the cheek.

It brought tears to Max's eyes. He loved this little boy so much, and was sorry he had missed his first years – but so glad he was with him now. He had told Sam on the way home that he wanted to save the cinema trip for Saturday so that Auntie Lar could come. Sam had asked him if he wanted Auntie Lar for a girlfriend, and Max had thrown his head back, laughed, and said, "Maybe, but it's a secret, ok?"

"Ok," said Sam, "but girls are yucky – I'll never have a girlfriend." Max just looked at him and smiled.

****

When Mia came in at 11.30, she was smiling to herself. She was so happy – the evening had gone brilliantly. Brian had told her that he'd noticed her as soon as she started her job, but was too embarrassed to say anything to her. He watched her from a distance every day, but he was afraid she would rebuff him if he asked her out. In addition, he didn't want to ask her while she was still mourning for Bonnie. During the last few days she had looked happier, and he finally asked her out on impulse.

Well, she was very glad he had. She was now feeling warm all over. She was seeing him again in two days for another date. She had never felt like this before. He had kissed her and she had melted. She didn't think she would sleep at all tonight.

Laura ran towards her, demanding a full report on the evening. They sat up chatting in the kitchen until the early hours, and Laura told Mia she was going to the cinema and lunch tomorrow with Max and Sam. Mia could see this relationship coming together nicely.

***

Laura lay in bed thinking about Max and her feelings for him; it was very peaceful in her bedroom. She had decorated it in soft pink, and she loved it. James had hated it, but she was glad she'd stuck to her guns. It was done out in soft pastels with butterfly designs on the curtains. She loved this room. It backed onto the garden, and she loved the noise of the birds first thing in the morning. As she lay there reflecting, Bonnie's voice whispered her name. She sat up and answered.

"Bonnie, is that you?"

"Yes, who else would it be?" Bonnie replied. Laura laughed, and asked her what she wanted at this time of day.

"I want to talk to you – its better when you're quiet and peaceful."

"Ok, go ahead."

"Well, firstly, I want you to have a fantastic time tomorrow, and I don't want you to think of me. I'd love you to get together with Max. I can't turn the clock back, and you have to look forward."

"Secondly, I've seen mum."

"What!" Laura expostulated. "You said you hadn't – why did you lie?"

"I wasn't lying, Laura: I hadn't seen her when you asked me. It was a few days ago, and Rob took me over. I haven't really had a chance to tell you properly until now."

"How did she look? Please tell me."

"Ok, I'm about to. She looked amazing, and she told me to tell you how much she loved us all. She told me she's visited you a few times and that she was there for Sam's birth – which is amazing, because I felt so calm at the time. Her hair was dark brown, like when she first started her nursing, and she looked radiant and very happy. She also told me she was bringing Nan and granddad to meet me when I go back for good."

"What do you mean, 'for good'? Are you leaving?"

"Not quite yet, I hope – I'll let you know when. I'll just be around less and less until I'm just visiting occasionally."

***

All three girls had worshipped their mother Mary. She had been very attractive, with dark, curly hair, a heart-shaped face, and a wonderful personality. She had been thirty-two when her husband, in classic tabloid fashion, ran off with the woman next door. The girls were only little then. Laura remembered it with clarity though.

Mary's personality had changed overnight. She couldn't stand the thought of living next door to Martin, seeing him with "that tart" every day, or putting her children through the pain of seeing him. She grabbed everything she could carry and took the kids on the train up to Birmingham, then straight to the nearest police station. She told the desk officer a great lie: that she had run away from her abusive husband and needed somewhere to stay.

Mary had put on a very good show at the police station. She had warned the children, on the train up to Birmingham, to say nothing. The police had got her in touch with Birmingham social services and the city council, had put her in a hostel where she stayed for eight months until they re-housed her. She had struggled at times to bring the girls up on her own.

Once the children were in junior school, she went to college for twelve months, then university for three years, and finally became a qualified nurse. It took her five years, and every day was a struggle. By the time she qualified, the girls were in senior school, and their new independence finally allowed her to earn a full-time wage. At last, Mary had been able to spoil her children with lovely gifts and days out. Every weekend they went out to eat. In the summer, they spent two weeks down in Cornwall. They always went back to the same place: it had become their haven, and they looked forward to it every year.

The girls had a great time growing up with their mum, and she filled all their time up with activities and clubs.

Mary had died five years ago after a massive heart attack. It had knocked the girls for six: all those years of struggling, and now she was gone ... it was inconceivable that it could have happened. Mary had never had health problems before – she never smoked. It took the girls more than a year to get over her death.

Therefore, Laura was in very low spirits when she met her future husband James. He had seen her sitting on a park bench looking unhappy, and had sat down next to her. They got talking, sitting together for hours before realising what time it was ... and a relationship got off the ground. Eighteen months later, they had married. She thought about him a lot ... but not with as much love as she thought she should feel.

Laura shook herself: all these memories would make her feel worse if she carried on.

Laura pondered for a while, and then realised she wanted to ask Bonnie to find out something.

"Please ask Rob if there's any chance whatsoever that I could come and visit mum – just once and just long enough for a hug and kiss."

"It's impossible, I think, Laura."

"Even if he lets mum come to see me would be good. Please Bonnie."

"I'm not sure Laura"

"Please, just ask him, Bonnie."

"Ok, I'll ask, but please don't expect

anything."

When Bonnie saw Rob, he just looked at her and told her he knew what Laura had requested: he was in the room at the time, invisible to either of them. Rob explained that the only way he thought a visit could happen was in a dream: they could take Laura for a visit if she was in a dream state, but she may not remember it.

Bonnie thought that any visit would be detrimental for Laura's healing, and she was sure that Laura would appreciate it very much.

"What about Mia? We are forgetting that your mother had *three* daughters. She'd be terribly hurt if we did this without her knowledge."

"I think you should speak to both of your sisters, and allow them both the opportunity to talk: if one remembers the dream then so be it, but hopefully they both will; I'll sort it out nearer the time of your departure – that way your sisters will find it easier to let you go."

Bonnie looked troubled, and Rob asked her why.

"The only thing I'm worried about is Mia's baby. Mum had the baby with her: if Mia meets her baby daughter she may suffer when she recognises her – she could become depressed, and that worries me."

"Don't worry, my dear, I'll make sure everything works out to keep everyone happy."

*** *** ***

Laura, Max and Sam had a fantastic time on Saturday. They went to see Shrek, and Sam loved it. Max grabbed Laura's hand halfway through the film. She had gone crimson and was glad it was dark. Her heart was beating at a hundred miles an hour and she felt clammy, but at the same time she felt ecstatic .

When the film finished they went to one of the diners, which were scattered around the cinema complex. Laura usually refused to buy Sam "takeaway rubbish", as she called it, and in the film, she had allowed him only a small packet of Maltesers – she was very protective of him, and wanted him to have a good diet. Now she relented. They all sat with plates of pizza and chips in front of them, talking about the film. Even Max and Laura had found parts of it entertaining, and they agreed to take Sam again if another film came out suitable for his age.

Max kept looking over his plate and watching Laura. He thought to himself, "I could grow to love this woman." When they got home Sam was exhausted, and he didn't complain once about being washed and going to bed. His eyes closed as soon as his head hit the pillow.

Max went downstairs after tucking Sam in, and poured two glasses of wine. He sat with Laura and chatted easily about their day, and about Sam and nursery. Laura couldn't look him in the face for fear she would go red, but the wine relaxed her and they had a pleasant evening.

On Sunday they all went to the park and took Sam on the boating lake. It was a lovely day. Of course, halfway round the lake Bonnie said "Boo!" and laughed. Laura and Max jumped, and Max dropped an oar in the water. He reached over and grabbed it quickly, but he got his shirt soaked in the process. Mia, as always, just looked amused. She knew it was Bonnie. "Here we go again," said Laura, laughing. "You really are a swine." Sam asked her why she was calling his daddy a swine; she couldn't be bothered to explain, so she said she meant "a swan", and pointed to the majestic birds on the river bank.

"Oh," said Sam, "but it wasn't the swan's fault that daddy dropped the boat mover into the water." Laura laughed and said she knew that, and the boat mover was called an "oar", and no, it wasn't his daddy's fault. She hadn't heard him call him daddy before and it felt good: he deserved it. He had spent every waking moment since he met Sam with him, when he wasn't at work.

They had had a lovely day, and a pleasant evening. When Sam was put to bed later, they sat and played Sorry! It made them all laugh and jump when each of them shouted. "Gosh, Mia, you'll wake Sam up in a minute," Laura said.

"No I won't," she replied. "He's shattered – he's had a long day," which was true, and they all retired early anyway. They were all tired. It had been a lovely enjoyable day. Max and Mia had work the next day, and Laura had to get up early to prepare Sam for nursery.

CHAPTER 11

Max was at work. He had arranged to take the last three weeks off, but now he was back. His manager Steve had reduced his hours for him, so as long as he was in at six each morning he could finish work at three in the afternoon. It gave him chance to pick Sam up from nursery at three-thirty. Laura let him use the shower at the house. He had stayed at the house for tea the last two days. After showering, he stayed for the rest of the afternoon. He could play with Sam and put him to bed. He had grown to love him so much that he hated being away from him. He had told Sam he was his daddy a few days ago. He didn't know how much Sam understood, but he had said, "Goodnight, daddy" last night, and Max had felt that lovely feeling again like he did on the boating lake.

Max was working on a building development which would take at least six months to complete – he was glad about the timescale. When they changed sites, he didn't know how far he would be from the nursery. However, for now he was happy.

At that moment, a massive roar enveloped him, and he felt his ears almost explode. The sound seemed to go on for ages, although it probably lasted only seconds. The pain in his ears was immense. He put his hands over his ears and tried to shout, but there was no way he could be heard. Dust and rubble started to hit him; he dropped down and covered his head. He managed to move back slightly, but bricks were bouncing off him. He then heard shouting, crying, and then more roaring. He was covered in dust and couldn't see: his eyes were full of dust, and tears were streaming down his face from the stinging.

More bricks were hitting him. He tried to crawl away, and he could hear people shouting his name. Rubble and dust was falling, a large pile of debris fell on his leg, and he screamed in pain. Then another brick landed on his arm. He felt himself being pushed really hard and he landed sideways. A single brick finally landed on his head, and then there was darkness.

*** *** ***

Laura was beside herself. The hospital had found her number in the mobile phone that Max had in his pocket. Her number was the first to answer. She had called Mia to come from work and was driving towards Merrifield hospital. Apparently, Max was unconscious, with head injuries and a broken leg. They had operated on his leg and it would have to be pinned. She couldn't believe it. She rang Marie and asked her to pick up Sam and look after him until one of them could get home.

They parked in a disabled bay and did not care; it was worth a ticket if they got one, because it was close to the entrance. Laura ran to the reception and asked where she could find Max Collins. The receptionist gave them directions to ward three, and they caught the lift up. Mia told Laura not to worry too much.

Laura heard Bonnie whisper, "Don't worry too much. Rob's told me Max will be ok."

"So what happened to angels and all that protecting you then?" said Laura. Mia gave Laura a quizzical look and said, "I don't know."

116

"I wasn't talking to you," replied Laura. "I was talking to Bonnie."

"Well, excuse me if I thought it was me you were talking to, considering there's only two of us in the blooming lift!"

Laura looked at Mia and panting said, "I'm sorry, love."

Laura said to Mia, "Bonnie whispered to me again. I'm all at sixes and sevens."

Then Bonnie whispered in Laura's ear again. "Look, we can't change the way of life people lead. Rob said your angels are with you everywhere you go, but they can't change what's coming to you: they can protect you if you ask them to – but only if it's for your own good."

"Oh, that's all right then," said Laura out loud. "A few bricks fall on your head and it's ok because it was meant to happen. It was for his own bloody good that he got knocked out and broke his leg?"

Bonnie said. "His angel did help him. Rob

said he's met him and he's met both of your angels too, I'll tell you about it later."

The lift doors opened and the girls went to the nurses' station to enquire about Max. The nurse led them to his bed and told them he was still unconscious at the moment but all the signs were fine and the doctor would be around shortly. The nurse told them they could talk to Max, but they could only stay for thirty minutes.

Max looked very pale – almost wax-like. His head was heavily bandaged. He had small cuts all over his face. His leg was in plaster, and elevated. He had perforated eardrums, which made it hard for him to hear, and his arms were covered in large dressings. Laura started crying and grabbed his hand. Mia told her to calm down, as they didn't want him to wake and see her upset.

Twenty minutes later Max started to stir and both girls lent over him, calling his name. The nurse came running over and asked them to stand back. She checked his fluids and shone a light in his eyes, which made him wince.

"The doctor will be in to see you soon, Mr Collins."

Max was aware, but not fully awake. He felt tired, and his ears were painful. He could feel a dull, throbbing pain in his leg, and he tried to shout out. The nurse asked the girls to step outside for a moment and she showed Max how to use his pain relief button, which was attached to a syringe that gave pain relief on demand. When he seemed calmer, she told him he had visitors and they could come back in, but only stay for a few more minutes. She called the girls in and explained that they had a short time with Max. Laura sat on one side and Mia on the other. Max looked at both of them in turn and said.

 "I'm lucky to have lovely women on both sides of me."

He sounded really hoarse and tired. They both kissed him on the forehead and said they would visit tomorrow. Max relaxed onto his pillow and slipped into a deep sleep. The nurse explained that this was normal and the girls should let him rest: hopefully he would look better tomorrow.

Laura was relieved that he had woken up, and she asked the nurse if she could speak to the doctor before she left. Just as she was speaking to the nurse, the doctor came in and asked if she was a relative. She explained who she was and told him that she had telephoned his brother: his parents lived over four hundred miles away and were elderly. She had told his brother to let them know. She didn't have their details, anyway. She only found his brother's phone number when she went through his bag, which he left at her house yesterday.

The girls sat sipping hot chocolate in the hospital canteen.

"I hope he's going to be ok. Sam will be upset when we tell him."

"Well, we need only tell him that he's had an accident and is going to be ok."

The girls spent the next few days going to and from the hospital. They took Sam on the fourth day, when Max was looking a lot better, so as not to scare him too much. They explained to Sam that he couldn't jump on Max or he would hurt him: so now, Sam was being extra gentle.

Laura was devastated. She knew now that she was in love with Max: as soon as the hospital had telephoned, she had known. Her heart had felt as though it was going to pound out of her chest. She had started shaking and crying. They had told her that Max had been in a construction accident and was in theatre as they spoke – but they couldn't tell her how serious it was, so her mind had gone into overdrive, thinking the worst.

There was no way that Max could return to his flat because of the stairs, and he would need some help with washing. Laura had made arrangements for Max to come and stay at her house while he was recuperating. His leg had the worst injury, and he would need follow-up appointments for at least three months. The only good aspect for Max was that he would see Sam and Laura every day. He knew he was falling in love with her, but she was Bonnie's sister and he was guilty for feeling so strongly about her.

Laura was looking forward to playing nursemaid. Mia had let her single bed be brought downstairs for him, and she was going to treat herself to a double bed. The room she was in was big enough to accommodate one. Sam was also excited to be having his daddy come to live with them, although he was upset when he heard he'd had the accident. Sam had cheered up as soon as he had seen his daddy smiling.

Max spent five days in the hospital before he was discharged. The doctors had told him he was extremely lucky to have come out of the accident with only slight concussion and a broken leg. The amount of rubble, which had fallen, could have killed a man. Max remembered the massive shove he had felt before he was knocked out, and he was sure it had been Bonnie saving him.

Max sat with the girls on his first evening home and, once his painkillers had taken effect, he told them what had happened at the site. Apparently, a large number of cement bags and bricks had been sitting on the scaffolding above him and one of the wooden planks had collapsed, sending all the materials down on him. As he was talking he became pensive, and Laura asked him if he was ok.

"You don't have to talk about it, Max."

"No!" replied Max. "It's fine, but I want to tell you that someone pushed me out of the way. I know I didn't imagine it, I promise. It was after my leg was hit – it was a massive push: do you think it was Bonnie?"

Laura told him what Bonnie had said in the lift about everyone having angels, and that Rob had met Max's angel, who had told him that he had been there and helped him.

"Wow, that is amazing!" said Max. I thought I was going mad for a while, but then I think I have been since Bonnie spoke to me!" He gave a chuckle.

Max's manager at the site had told him he would get full pay for six months while he was off work, and that he was sorting him out a compensation claim through the company's insurers. He wasn't to worry how long it took for him to get well.

CHAPTER 12

Bonnie had been on a journey of her own. Rob had taught her such a lot. He had taken her into all sorts of situations. Everything he taught her was to make her transition easier.

She had been to see babies being born in all sorts of places, from China to Rotherham to Egypt, and every time she had watched a child being born, she had seen that baby's angel by its side. She was amazed.

She had also seen accidents, and watched while angels escorted the deceased victims to wherever they were being taken. She realised now that dying was not as straightforward as it had seemed. She had watched many different decisions made by people, and then Rob had allowed her to see the outcomes. Some were good, others bad. It taught her about the paths people take in life, and what they choose for themselves.

Rob explained other things to her about being selfish and spiteful. He told her the only way to be happy is to love. "That's what life is about, Bonnie: just love, pure love, will bring happiness. People should just love each other, and learn to forgive. Once you forgive, your heart lifts and you are free of bad feeling, which allows room for more love. Being gentle, loving, and caring is the way forward. If people become like that, they will learn lessons even from their own unhappiness."

"But how will people know?"

"They should feel it, Bonnie," Rob replied. "When you do something good for others, no matter what it is, you feel wonderful inside: you positively glow. That is pure love enveloping you, so you should learn from it and keep those feelings coming. Just helping someone out or visiting someone who is lonely is enough to produce the love. There aren't many people who can live without that feeling. Come, Bonnie, I'll show you."

She felt herself spinning, and she was off again. She was now looking down on a disaster area. Rob was pointing at someone, and she noticed a man digging through rubble. All of a sudden, she watched as he pulled a bleeding child from the debris and started running with it towards a large green tent. Rob told her that the man in question spends all his time volunteering and that he goes wherever there is need.

"Although the child was crying, the man's face was alight – did you notice?"

"Yes I did. I'm starting to understand more – I just wish I'd known all this when I was alive."

"But you did, my dear – you just decided not to do anything about it. Every last one of us, when on the earth, can feel that love inside us." Bonnie looked unsure.

"But if everyone felt like that, wouldn't we all have gone to different countries to save people?"

"No, it doesn't work like that. We can make a difference in any country: just a phone call can make someone happy. There are hundreds of ways that people can feel good about themselves – they just need to realise it. We spend our lives collecting things around us and being greedy, without realising that we need to own very little."

When she wasn't with Rob, Bonnie was still spending a lot of time around the girls and Sam, but she wasn't communicating so much: she thought they had enough to contend with, since Max had his accident.

A few weeks later Laura and Mia were sitting with Max, watching the news, when Bonnie said, "Hi guys." Max and Laura automatically jumped apart, and Mia gave them a knowing look.

"Hi, Bonnie," Laura Saïd out loud. "Where have you been?"

"I've been with Rob. You could say it was a field trip. It's like being back at school."

Laura and Max laughed. Mia looked annoyed, then Bonnie lightly laid her hands on her shoulder again, and her face changed. Bonnie stayed there for a long while, and Laura and Max knew that Mia had been touched: her eyes were gleaming. Max and Laura smiled at each other. Bonnie said out loud, "I know you've fallen in love with each other, and you have my blessing. I promise you I'm very happy." Laura spluttered and Max suffered the shame of going red himself. They didn't know which way to turn and couldn't look each other in the face. Bonnie gave a wicked giggle.

Mia decided there and then never to complain about not hearing Bonnie: she would much prefer that feeling of love that she received when Bonnie touched her, rather than being made to jump every two minutes!

Max asked Laura if they could go for a walk somewhere. Mia smiled, "Carry on – I'll be there if Sam wakes up."

They slowly walked through the square, then towards the village. It was peaceful and quiet. It was quite difficult for Max to walk with the crutches, but the doctors had told him he needed to exercise his leg as much as possible. The more he did for himself now, the less physiotherapy he would need later. The last scan had shown that it was healing well and the pins were placed perfectly.

It was quite breezy, so they decided to stop at

a local coffee house. It served delicious coffees and teas, and Laura and Mia had often sat chatting over coffee there.

"Hello, my lovely." Shirley, the owner, was a large, happy lady who never seemed to stop working. She pulled out a chair for Max, and helped him to settle into a seat. She took his crutches off him and leant them against the wall.

"Thank you very much," Max said.

"What can I get you both?"

"Two of your special coffees, please," replied Laura.

"I haven't seen you here in a while. How's Mia, and that dear little chap?"

Laura gave her a big smile. "They are both fine and Sam is getting bigger by the day."

She introduced Max as Sam's father gave her a cheeky wink and said, "I will catch up with you later when Mia is free."

"Ok, my dear, enjoy your drinks." She

looked Max up and down and winked at Laura, who immediately went red and let her head drop.

Max was feeling tongue-tied, but decided to spill the beans. Once they had ordered Max told her that he had fallen in love with her, as Bonnie had said. She wasn't to worry if she didn't feel the same. Laura felt the blood rush up her neck and into her face. Looking down, she told him she felt the same. Max put his finger under her chin and lifted her head.

"Repeat what you just said."

"I feel the same," she whispered. "Why do you think I can't speak properly when you're around, and why does my face burn up the minute you speak to me?" Max leant over the table, grabbed her hands, pulled her close, and kissed her. Max would have jumped with joy but was unable to, his leg being so painful. Bonnie felt her heart leap and she became warm from the top of her head to her toes. Now she knew what it meant when people talked about your toes curling. She kissed him back and felt like never stopping. She had never, ever felt like this when James kissed her, even in the beginning. Laura could feel Shirley's eyes on her and she wanted nothing more than to go home and continue what they had started…

They called a cab to get back, because Laura thought it would be too much for Max to walk back with the crutches. They held hands in the taxi, and when they arrived at the house, Mia was watching out of the window. She was worried at first, thinking Max had fallen or hurt himself, but once they got out and she saw them holding hands and looking loved-up she knew they had told each other how they felt. She had known for a while – you couldn't miss the way they looked at each other when the other one wasn't looking. It made her smile; she hoped she would feel that way about someone one day.

CHAPTER 13

Bonnie had watched the happenings in the coffee shop and kept quiet. She was glowing with happiness. She now knew she could go soon. She felt in her heart that everything would be ok. Her little boy had a new mummy, his daddy, and his auntie. He would grow up well-adjusted and happy, and that was what she cared about most.

Rob touched Bonnie's shoulder, "You're happy now, aren't you, Bonnie?"

"Yes I am but I would like to see Mia settled too." Rob laughed.

"That my dear, might take a while."

Bonnie smiled.

"Hey Rob," Bonnie chuckled. "Maybe it's any excuse to stay for a while." They both grinned.

Max and Laura spent the next few weeks driving Mia mad. Once Sam was at nursery they were hugging, kissing, and getting to know one another, and showing themselves in a totally new light. Mia was glad she was at work most of the time – they were driving her nuts!

Laura received her divorce papers through the post, and she had signed them and sent them back immediately. She was in no rush anyway. She loved Rob but didn't want to get married again. Well, she didn't feel like it now, that was for sure.

Mia also enjoyed life. She was happy for Laura and Max, and she had plenty to occupy her mind now with Brian. They spent many evenings' together and visited different places, including the art gallery and the museum – not that she was looking at art much: she was too engrossed in being with Brian. He really was a dream.

Mia had quite enjoyed the art gallery and just strolling around in the peaceful atmosphere had an effect on her. A lot of the work they were seeing was historical and bored her somewhat, but linking arms with Brian sent a thrill through her, that conversation was not needed. She found the Tempera collection of art was the most interesting.

"I like the colours in this collection"

"I was thinking the same." Brian replied

"The rest bored me though," Mia stated with a grin on her face.

"We must be psychic," laughed Brian. Mia laughed at the very idea, if only he knew.

Bonnie, now sure that Laura and Rob were suited, was spending time at Sam's nursery, and with Mia and Brian. But she was getting weaker in her communications, and when she was speaking to Laura she wasn't getting through as easily as before. She could normally speak to her at any time, but lately she had to speak when Laura was just about to sleep. It was keeping Laura awake though so she would speak to Rob soon, and find out why she was fading.

Laura and Rob had started walking a lot. The doctors had told Rob the more exercise he did the better, so they both bought a good pair of running shoes to go on long walks together: and the times that they were able to walk were increasing. The first time they went out, Rob was in agony after fifteen minutes so they had returned home; but after two weeks, they were managing to walk for over half an hour. They both came in looking slightly dishevelled and red from their exertions. Laura had jogged slowly, while Rob had walked. He was getting healthier all the time.

"We'll both be jogging in six months," Rob said. Laura agreed, and told him he was doing fantastically. She stretched up and placed a kiss on the end of his nose. Max put his arms around Laura. "I love you."

Laura told him to go and have a shower while she peeled some potatoes ready for tea. It was two o'clock in the afternoon already, and if he looked at her like that again, she may just rip his clothes off. Sam would be coming home at half past three, and she hadn't got tea started yet.

"Have we got time? I need you to help me

change my trousers." Max squinted down at her. Laura laughed up at his mischievous face, and said he could change them himself. She knew exactly what was on his mind.

Mia would be picking Sam up today on her way home from work so she needed to hurry.

Bonnie was at Sam's nursery, watching him. Her love for him was overwhelming. She gazed at his lovely face and noticed his hair, with wispy curls around his ears; she used to twirl them in her fingers while he fell asleep on her, and soon afterwards, she had noticed him doing it himself. She used to think that she would never get them cut off, but now he was growing he was starting to look girlish. She would have a word with Laura later. Sam was chatting to his friend, who was telling him to do something. Bonnie couldn't hear clearly but she saw Sam shake his head. The boy carried on whispering to Sam. All the children were sitting in a circle ready for a story. They were giggling and fidgeting. Then the teacher asked them to be quiet and still. They all sat up straight and stopped chattering.

There was a sharp knock on the door and another teacher beckoned to Miss Lawson to come out. As she was leaving, she turned to all the children and asked them to sit nicely: she would be back in a moment. Just then, the little boy next to Sam nudged him and pointed to the corner of the room.

As Bonnie looked over, she knew immediately what was going on. On top of the filing cabinet at the far side of the room sat a teddy bear holding a large chocolate bar. It was for the end of term competition. Bonnie rushed over to Sam and said, "Don't you dare!" Sam was already on his feet, and Bonnie started shouting, "stop Sam stop." but he wasn't listening. Bonnie became frantic. She tried to touch him, but her hand went straight through him. Now she was scared, and trying desperately to talk.

She attempted to calm herself and concentrate. She kept repeating his name – "Sam, Sam, please listen" – but he had now climbed to the top of the cabinet. He grabbed the bear, held it tight, and tried to get down. The other children were giggling and pointing at Sam. Bonnie could have smacked the little boy at that moment: her son was in danger, and she was so worried. "Where's that teacher?" she thought. She wanted to look, but didn't want to leave Sam at that moment.

All of a sudden there was an ear-splitting metallic noise as the filing cabinet came crashing down. The children started screaming and crying, and Sam was yelling too – he was stuck under the cabinet. Bonnie was trying to move it, but nothing was happening: she was weak, and she knew it. She was scared, and felt her heart pounding. Yet she felt in that moment very much alive.

The teacher, hearing the commotion, came running in. She had been gone less than two minutes. She picked the cabinet up with the help of her colleague. Sam was free, but injured quite badly: one of his legs was bent at a peculiar angle, and he was white in the face. He was whimpering.

Bonnie felt helpless. She thought of Laura and said to herself, "Yes, Laura." She concentrated on Laura and found herself in Laura's kitchen.

Rob was standing there.

"Why weren't you with me!?" she shouted at him. "Sam is injured – he needs help now!"

"Don't worry, Bonnie – the ambulance is on its way."

"Why can't anyone hear me, Rob?"

"It's because you're fading, my dear: it will soon be time to go."

"No!" shouted Bonnie. "Not yet! Please, no!"

She started shouting "Laura", and Laura turned just for a moment, as if she may have heard her. She shouted her name again, but nothing happened. Bonnie started shouting again, "Please, Laura, please! Sam needs you; hear me, oh, please hear me."

Rob just shook his head sadly. Bonnie looked at Laura and started running towards her. Rob shouted, "No, Bonnie! "Ignoring him, she jumped – and landed inside Laura, she started to move.

Laura jumped, feeling she had received an

electric shock. Then she ran into the hall and grabbed her trainers. She had a powerful energy inside her.

"Whatever is happening to me?" she shouted. She didn't know why she had just run out of the house without any reason. She must be going mad, she thought. She ran down the road and kept going past the square. She was crying but didn't know why. She was running faster now, and knew she was running towards the nursery. Some sixth sense was telling her she was needed, so she started running even faster. Her heart was pounding. She was now on the Bristol Road. She carried on past the primary school. She could see the nursery in the distance. She saw an ambulance. She knew now it was for Sam, and she almost collapsed with anxiety. She managed to get to the entrance, but the security system locked her out. She couldn't breathe, so was unable to speak. She stood for a few moments to calm herself, then put her finger on the bell. She kept it there till the manager came out. As soon as he saw who it was, he opened the gate.

"Please come in; that was very quick, Mrs

Miller."

"What do you mean, that was quick? Where's Sam? I need to see him."

"He's in the ambulance. I rang your house and a gentleman answered and said you'd be right here – but it was only two minutes ago that I rang."

"Well, I had a feeling, so I came ahead."

"Max must have got in just after I left."

"Are you ok, my dear? You look terrible."

"Yes, I'm ok – I just need to see Sam." At that moment, Bonnie removed herself from Laura's body and ran to the ambulance. Laura collapsed onto the floor and took in lungs full of fresh air.

The manager astounded, ran over. "You need to be checked over Mrs Miller please"

"No I will be ok in a moment." Laura managed to regain her equilibrium and stood up. "God knows what happened there."

I think it's just shock Mrs Miller, please follow me. You may need to be checked over too – you really don't look well at all."

Sam was being given some gas and air through a mask for his pain. The paramedic explained that he had certainly broken one of his legs, and would need to go straight to the hospital. Laura jumped into the back of the ambulance, crying Sam's name. He heard her and looked over. His face was smeared with dirty tears, leaving long streaks down his face. He looked a forlorn little boy.

"I'm so sorry, Auntie Lar. I've been really naughty."

"Don't worry, my love – we're all naughty somctimes."

Laura grabbed Sam's hand and squeezed it. He looked at her and said, "Auntie Lar, it hurts."

"Ok, Sam my love, we'll get you better soon." She stayed with him in the ambulance, and rang Mia to tell her to meet her at the hospital. She then rang home, but there was no answer. Just as the ambulance doors were about to close, Max came running up and jumped in. He checked Sam and kissed his head.

"Ok, mate, everything's going to be ok."

"What happened, Laura?"

"Apparently he fell off a cabinet, and the cabinet landed on his legs." Max had tears falling down his face and he held Sam's hand tight all the way to the hospital. Max was petrified. Bonnie was also in the ambulance, and Rob was by her side.

"I'm not ready, Rob – this has proved it. Please: I need to stay. I need you to just give me a while longer. I can't do with fading away: it's not fair on me, and it's not fair on the girls or Sam. They must think I've abandoned them."

Rob looked at Bonnie's sad face and told her he would speak to his "Highers".

"What do you mean by your 'Highers'?" Rob smiled.

"The angels that are higher than me. I'll get back to you." Bonnie was stroking Sam's hair.

She knew he couldn't feel her not now, and she was upset. If there was any time he had needed to feel her, it would have been now.

She called Rob in her mind, and he appeared.

"Why now, please, tell me Rob, why?" Rob looked upset for her.

"It's very hard for you, I know Bonnie, but this was meant to happen."

"My little boy is in agony – how can this be?"

"How can this be? What's meant to happen? Rob, please, I need to know." Rob looked at Bonnie's distraught face.

"Ok Bonnic, I'll tell you. Calm down and listen carefully. Nobody gets insights into anyone's life as I am about to give you. Normally you would only find these things out when you die. What I'm about to tell you is a small percentage of what you'll learn when you pass over."

"When Sam is older, he will have a large group of friends. At the age of thirteen, he'll be with a group of boys who climb a dangerous building. Sam will walk away because he's scared of heights, and the reason he is scared of heights is because of an accident that he had at the age of three. One of his friends that day will lose his life. You must remember, Bonnie, that there is a reason for everything. But Sam will not die young, this I can tell you."

"Oh my God, I can't believe this – I can't take it all in."

Rob put his arms around Bonnie and let his love and kindness flow through her. At that moment, she understood, although at this time she couldn't clarify to herself what she understood she just had a feeling of peace and knowing. It was all very confusing. She looked puzzled. Rob told her to try to calm herself, and said he would come and see her later.

Bonnie stayed with Sam throughout his ordeal, and although he would not know she was there, it comforted her to be with him.

Once at the hospital, Sam was taken straight to theatre. It was obvious from the state of his legs that he had broken at least one: it was at a strange angle; and the other one was very swollen.

Laura and Max sat in the waiting area. They had both given Sam a kiss and told him to be brave, and that they would be outside as soon as he had "got mended".

Sam was keen on superheroes these days, so they told him how powerful he was. He even managed a smile before he was put to sleep.

Mia came running in, and they explained what had happened.

Laura and Mia found themselves in the same position, as they had been when they were waiting for the result of Max's accident.

"I'm fed up of this hospital Mia," Laura mumbled.

Mia just looked at Laura in amazement "Are you mad? We're all fed up of being here."

"I'm sorry," Laura replied. "We're all in the same boat, I know, but I'm so worried about Sam, and I haven't heard from Bonnie. I feel that it's entirely my fault. He was left in my care, and now look what's happened."

"Don't be silly Laura, of course it's not our fault. He was at nursery when it happened – but yes, I'm anxious about Bonnie too. I haven't felt her either and it's making me uneasy."

Max had neither felt nor heard from Bonnie for a while, and it troubled him too.

CHAPTER 14

Bonnie was sitting next to Sam, stroking his arm. He was still sedated from his operation. They had put his broken leg in plaster. The other leg had no fractures but there was some tissue damage, hence the swelling. He just needed plenty of rest and physiotherapy. The only good thing about being dead, Bonnie thought, was that she could hear what the doctors were saying and they couldn't see her.

Rob appeared by her side, and she asked him instantly if he had sorted it out for her to stay longer. He replied with a smile and a nod, and Bonnie jumped up and put her arms around him. "You feel so solid and real, is that normal?"

"Yes Bonnie its normal. "Look, you'll have more time, my dear, but it's not long. You'll be stronger now, and you must be careful because Sam will see you again."

Bonnie thought of Laura and Mia, and found herself next to them in the waiting area.

"Hi, Laura," Bonnie said, quite loudly. She was so excited to be able to get through that she forgot to whisper. Laura jumped and spilt her coffee on the floor.

"Bonnie, where have you been?" Laura whispered.

Mia looked up. "Is she here? Where has she been? Ask her."

Bonnie told Laura she had heard her. She explained what had happened, and that she had been fading for a few days, but she had now sorted it out and would be able to tell everyone before she was to go.

"I'm so sorry about Sam Laura said.

"Don't worry. I know the reason behind it and he is going to be fine." Laura's face looked haggard and her mouth opened like a fish taking gulps of oxygen.

"What's going on Laura?" Mia said shaking Laura's shoulder, what's wrong?"

"Bonnie's just told me there was a reason why Sam hurt himself."

"Wow," Mia replied with a sarcastic smile. "So every time people get hurt, there's a reason? Well, what a load of claptrap. My little nephew is in agony, but there's a reason?"

Bonnie spoke again to Laura "I felt the same, it's all been explained, and I'm at ease with the situation."

"Well, would you like to enlighten us?" Rob shook his head at Bonnie,

"I'm not allowed to. Sorry."

Bonnie felt she was in the wrong place, and although she had understanding, the living never would, not until it was their time to go. No matter what she told a living person, they really did have to experience this for themselves. The less said by her the better, she would stay long enough to see them settled, and then she would go back to her mom where she belonged. Rob had promised her she would be happy and free.

***

Sam woke up the next day on the ward. He had been moved from the intensive care unit, and was feeling ok. He had no pain now and said he was comfortable. He gazed around at his environment, studying the pictures on the walls.

Opposite him were Disney characters; some he knew, and some, he didn't. On the ceiling was a picture of Superman flying through clouds. He thought it was brilliant. The best picture was one of Spiderman climbing the wall next to him. Whoever had painted the picture was very clever. It looked almost real. Spiderman was gazing over his shoulder, and it looked as though he was looking down on Sam.

Sam heard a sound and looked down towards his feet. There, sitting on the end of his bed, was his mummy.

"Wow! Hello mummy!" Bonnie looked at her cherub of a child and spoke.

"Hello darling, how are you? Are you in pain?"

"No, I'm fine, and look at these great pictures."

"I'm going to be a superhero when I'm big."

"I'm sure you will, poppet," his mom told him. Sam was a little worried. He spoke about his concerns to his mummy. He hadn't seen her for a long time. He told her about his accident. She told him that she'd been there but wasn't able to help him. Sam looked puzzled and cocked his head to one side, as though he was deep in thought.

Bonnie told him that she'd run all the way to Auntie Lars's house and made Auntie Lar run all the way to the nursery, puffing and panting. Sam giggled, imagining his auntie puffing and panting. Bonnie sat with Sam for quite a while, explaining little things in a way she thought he would understand.

Bonnie told him that she would be visiting less and less, until she did not appear to him at all. She told him she was leaving for heaven soon, but she would watch over him from heaven, and she would send him many angel kisses. Bonnie gazed into his angelic face; she brought her hand up and gently touched his cheek. Sam, acting a lot older than his years, told her that it was ok, that he was happy with his aunts. Then he started to point to the pictures on the wall.

Bonnie felt a little sad that Sam didn't seem to mind that she was going, but was also happy that he was settled.

The door to Sam's room opened, and a very pretty woman came and stood at the side of Sam's bed.

"Hi Sam," she said, "My name is Lucy, and I'm here to do some exercises with your leg." Sam's face dropped, and he was about to cry.

"Don't worry, it's not your bad one, it's the one with the bad muscles in," Lucy said, after seeing his face drop.

Lucy brought with her a special rolled-up cushion to roll out on the floor for the session. "We need to make sure that one leg gets better ready for when the other one is mended."

Sam was acquiescent, and Lucy was quite

shocked when he just said, "Ok, then." He looked up.

"You don't mind if my mum stops as well, do you?" Lucy knew Sam's background, and about his aunts who were bringing him up after his mother's death. Lucy was not sure how to answer this little boy, so she nodded.

"That will be fine."

"Good," shouted Sam, "cause she's here anyway!" he laughed, his blue eyes twinkling at her. She looked at him in amazement, then he gave her a toothy grin. He was adorable, and if he wanted to think his mom was there then it was fine by her. Bonnie watched Sam doing his exercises. He was faring quite well. "What a little minx!" she thought.

He was growing up quickly. Sam looked over at Bonnie, who was sitting on the end of his bed. He said, "I'm doing well, aren't I mummy?" Lucy looked to where Sam was looking: he was now having a conversation with an imaginary mother, but he was using facial expressions as you would in a real conversation.

She watched him for a while, and a few minutes later, she asked him what his mother had said. He replied that she had told him to work very hard for the nice lady so he could become stronger. Lucy looked at him in bewilderment; she hadn't expected that answer. Sam then told Lucy, "After a while I won't be seeing mummy any more. She's got to go and live with my granny in heaven, but she might pop back occasionally to watch over me."

Lucy was astounded that a little boy of three could talk this way: she almost believed him. Sam carried on doing the exercises Lucy was doing with him, but it was hurting a lot now. Bonnie placed her hand on his leg, and the pain went away. Sam said, "Thank you mummy." Lucy looked at him under her eyelashes. Sam looked up and gave her a lovely smile. He told her his mummy had just put her hand on his leg, and the pain had gone away. When Lucy looked down, the swelling on his left leg was almost gone. Lucy's eyes were almost popping out of her head in astonishment. She was now feeling scared. She tried to stand up, but found her legs were like jelly.

"Come on, Sam, I'll take you back to your bed." Sam was pleased it was over.

"Ok, can I have jelly and ice cream, please?" Who could refuse this little one? She thought.

"I'll ask the nurse for you. Now, you be a good boy and I'll see you tomorrow." Lucy picked Sam up and placed him on his bed. She covered him up and put his leg back in traction.

**

"Rob, where are you?" Bonnie whispered softly. She was outside the hospital, just gliding along. She hadn't thought herself anywhere; she just wanted time to think. She knew Sam was going to be ok. As always, Rob was correct.

"I'm here, Bonnie."

"Oh, hi Rob. We need to talk!"

"Yes, I think we do."

"Well, can I say what's on my mind first?"

"You usually do, my dear," replied Rob.

"Well, a while back, I asked about Laura and

Mia coming to visit mum, and you said it might be possible in a dream. I need to know more. I'm thinking I'm almost ready to stay with you. This will be my final wish. All of us suffered so much when mum died. I think it will leave my sisters at peace, knowing she is fine and happy."

Rob put his arms around Bonnie, and told her." I have something even better in mind: I have spoken to my Highers. I have permission, on this one occasion only, to actually take your sisters over to meet your mother. The one condition is that you cannot return with them."

"Oh my! ... Oh my! ... Oh my God! Rob, I'm so excited. I feel like crying. I'm flabbergasted. Bonnie started dancing around on the spot, then pulled Rob towards her, and started to dance around with him. A beautiful woman was watching them, and Bonnie waved. The woman waved back.

"Oh, bloody hell Rob, that woman just waved back at me."

"Bonnie, you need to stop taking the Lord's name in vain."

"I'm sorry Rob, I will try. I'm sorry. I mean it."

Rob knew she did, but also that it would keep happening. He smiled to himself.

"Ok, that lady you were waving at, she's in spirit like you."

"Why is she here then? I thought you weren't allowed to stay."

"Everyone has their own problems, and their own spirit guide. Her guide will sort her out. So stop worrying: you may not realise it, but probably thirty per cent of all the people you have walked or floated past have been spirits. They have their own journeys to undertake. You just worry about *your* journey, and what you're allowed to do – not what others are doing."

"I know, I know, I can't believe it! Can I tell them? Can I? Can I?"

"Calm down, Bonnie." He put his hand on her shoulder, and utter peace glided through her.

"Oh my!" She felt herself calming down.

"You are wonderful, Rob." Bonnie's eyes were misted over, as if she had been drugged. She was smiling, and looking so happy, but Rob needed her to be calm – otherwise she would scare her sisters to death. They wouldn't need a visit: they might drop dead with shock.

Mia and Laura had invited Brian round for tea. Mia hadn't seen him for a few days because of visiting Sam, but she'd missed him and he had phoned daily to see how she and Sam were. She was feeling serious about him. The more she spent time with him, the stronger her feelings became. Brian was also feeling the same, and unbeknown to Mia was preparing to propose. Mia wanted to sort things out with him. Brian was talking about buying a property, and when he mentioned it she had a feeling he was going to ask her to move in with him. Crazily, she was happy at Laura's, although Laura now had her man. Mia would soon be piggy-in-the-middle, so she had pondered for a while about bringing the subject up. If he asked her she would agree, as long as they lived within five minutes of Laura's. She knew this was selfish of her because he spoke of living closer to his work, but this was her life now and she needed to live it her way. She loved him, she knew that, but she would not compromise her love for Sam and Laura. She needed to be close. "Anyway," she thought, "I might be jumping the gun, and he might not ask me."

"Sam's coming home tomorrow," Laura told Mia when she came downstairs. The hospital just rang. He has to go back daily for physiotherapy, but it will only take half an hour so I'll take him and you can go back to work."

"Oh, ok," Mia said. She would be glad to get back to work. She had a backlog, and she had taken a week off while Sam was in hospital.

Max was still at the hospital, so Mia and Laura sat drinking coffee. Laura had just got changed and put some make-up on for the evening. It was the first meal they had organised for the four of them, so she wanted to make a good impression.

CHAPTER 15

Bonnie was sitting on the worn-out rocking chair, which no one would throw away, as it had been their grandfathers; and when Mary had passed away, the girls had inherited it. Mia had no room in her flat at the time, so it had been Laura who had been lumbered with it. "It's quite comfortable though," Bonnie thought, grinning like a Cheshire cat. She thought it was great not being seen. She watched the girls, and listened to them chatting about their men. "Yes!" she thought. "They're ok now." She knew what she was going to tell them would upset them, but she couldn't wait any longer.

"Laura!" Bonnie shouted. Laura jumped again, and yelped as the hot coffee spilt on the table and dripped down over the side onto her lap.

"Sorry."

"Sorry! How many times have you been told to whisper?" Bonnie apologised again.

"I was excited! I've got some important news."

"Oh, dammit, Bonnie," Laura cried out, as more coffee dribbled off the table and landed on her foot. Mia had jumped a mile when Laura burnt herself.

"Oh, so she's here, then!" Mia exclaimed, wiping the coffee up. Bonnie just gave her a look, and raised her eyes to the ceiling. Laura grabbed a pencil and paper, and told Mia to sit down.

"We'll see what this excitement is about. Pass that pad over, Mia." Laura made herself comfortable and was about to ask Bonnie to speak, when she heard a deep, gruff voice.

"Stop, wait – I'll do it!"

Mia jumped up, turning. She hit her head on the edge of the door. She looked at Laura.

"Who's that? I'm scared." Mia had never heard Bonnie speak, but she was hearing this voice and she was petrified.

"Sit!" the voice commanded. Both girls sat down. Mia was still rubbing the back of her head. Bonnie saw Rob, and said loudly, "All this time, and you haven't spoken to them. Why is there a need now?"

"There is a need. I'll explain everything."

Laura was glancing in all directions. She was hearing a man's voice, and Bonnie arguing with him. She had a feeling it was Rob, and it scared her. If Rob was speaking and she could hear it, there was something wrong. Laura started shaking.

"If anyone arrives while I'm speaking, I'll stop and come back another time. What I do or say can't be repeated, even to Max."

The girls sat and listened. They held hands tightly. They were both petrified, but wouldn't admit it. Hearing your sister was one thing, but hearing another dead person was terrifying. Holding tightly to each other, they heard Rob's voice.

"My name is Robert, and I'm Bonnie's spirit guide. I'm with her at all times while she is stuck here." The girls looked at each other, bewildered and very scared.

"Ok," they said in unison.

"A while back, in earth time, which I'll explain later, I took Bonnie to halfway heaven – that's what she likes to call it. She met your mother Mary." Mia just sat, open- mouthed. Her bottom lip was quivering like a child who was about to cry. Laura noticed and rubbed her hand. Bonnie came over and put her hand on Mia. The lovely peace-and-love feeling swam through Mia again, and she knew what Bonnie had done. She thanked her aloud, and relaxed.

"Bonnie has asked a special favour. I can honestly say it has never been granted before, so you're very special."

"What's that, then?" cried Laura.

"Wait – let me finish," Rob answered. "She wants me to take you to meet your mother."

There were gasps, and the girls looked at

each other in astonishment. Their mouths were moving, but no sounds emerged. Tears started to escape and run down Mia's face, which then triggered Laura's tears. Laura went starry-eyed, and thought she was going to collapse.

"Well, how can you do it, Will we die, What about Sam? No, no! I'm not going. Bonnie, what were you thinking?"

Both girls were shaking, and Rob put a hand on each of their shoulders. The girls felt it, and became peaceful immediately.

Rob said, "You see girls, imagine if I'd let Bonnie tell you all this: it wouldn't have gone down well, would it?" Both Laura and Mia understood, and said so. They both sat on the edge of the settee, and asked Rob to carry on.

"Now look," said Rob, "nothing bad will happen. You'll come back, but I'm afraid Bonnie won't. We've come to this compromise. You'll both come and visit, and when you leave, you'll be leaving alone."

"So we'll never hear or feel Bonnie again?"

"Well, there will be occasional visits, but she won't be around for long. She may come to check up on you. Once she reaches her realm, believe me, she won't want to come back."

"When will this happen, then?" Mia cried. Rob looked into Mia's eyes. They were shining with sorrow and excitement.

"We'll do it tomorrow, before Sam comes home. You'll need to make an excuse for Max to stay at the hospital with Sam. Mia, you'll need a few more days off work, I'm afraid."

"Why a few?"

"One for the visit, and one to get over it," Rob said, chuckling.

"I'll be back to see you tomorrow. That's enough for one day. Sleep well, my dears."

Rob left, chuckling to himself. Bonnie walked with Max out of the hospital gates. He was looking much happier since Sam's operation. She whispered his name quietly. She didn't want to cause him to panic, like she had done with Laura.

"Max!"

He lowered his head and quietly whispered.

"Yes, Bonnie."

"Let's turn right." He did so. They turned into a quiet road.

"I've just come to say goodbye. I'm leaving tomorrow, and I want to thank you for the love you've shown, Sam. I truly want you to know that I'm so very happy for you and Laura to be together."

"I love her," he told her. "I thought I was heartbroken when you left, and I actually think I was for a time, but I really do love her, Bonnie."

"Good, I'm glad. You deserve happiness, and who better to bring my little boy up than all three of you."

"Thank you, Laura. I still have deep feelings for you, and I always will. Do Laura and Mia know you're leaving?"

"Yes, they do, but I don't want you to

mention anything to them. They'll both be busy in the morning, so I'd like you to visit Sam in the morning, and you can bring him home when he's discharged."

"Will I never hear your voice again?" Max whispered sadly. Bonnie saw the sadness in his eyes, but she also knew that he had a lot to look forward to.

"I don't know yet if I'll be able to visit. If I am, whether I can be heard or not is another matter."

"This is goodbye, Max. I wish you all the best. Look after my baby and my sisters."

Max looked up into the clouds, and felt humble.

"I will, Bonnie, I promise. Good bye, Bonnie!"

Max spoke aloud, turning on the spot.
"Bonnie!" Bonnie!" There was no answer. He called her name again, but there was still no answer. Turning back, he started walking. He felt sad and happy, and a stray tear fell from his

eye. He wiped it away and started running towards Laura's house. He called it home now. He hadn't stayed at his own place for almost a month. They were having a meal tonight with Mia and Brian, and he had a feeling that something was going to happen. He could feel it in his bones. Laura and Mia were acting oddly yesterday. Well, as long as everyone was happy, then he was too.

*** *** ***

The girls had the house looking lovely, ready for the meal. They were chatting in the kitchen, and had opened a bottle of white wine. They were both excited, but fearful of tomorrow. Suddenly, Max came bounding in breathlessly. They both jumped up, alarmed.

"What on earth is the matter? Is Sam ok?" Laura cried.

"Oh, yes. Sorry, I just ran home from the hospital." He gave Laura a big hug, and a full kiss on the lips. Mia gave a loud tut and murmured about there being "a time and a place".

"So what have I done to deserve this, then?" Laura said. She tried to move over to the sink, with Max holding on to her.

"Nothing, honestly, but I need to tell you something." Laura looked into his eyes, and started to feel nervous.

"Come with me a minute."

"Ok. Where are we going?"

"Just to the front room," Max whispered.

Max held her hand, and declared, "I just want you to know how much I really love you. I was walking home from the hospital, and I just felt that my heart was full of love for you, so I started running. This intense love filled me, and I want you to know that I want to marry you, any time you want me."

"No, don't!" Max said, as Laura opened her mouth to protest. "I know you don't want to get married again, and I'm fine with that, but if you change your mind, I'll marry you. I just want you to know." Laura put her arms around him and nuzzled his neck.

"Now stop, or there will be no dinner tonight," Max said with a gruff voice. Laura laughed, and said, "Come on, you can help me. Brian will be here soon, and I need to get the dinner on. The starter's ready, but the main meal needs to go on now."

Brian knocked at the door, right on time. He had two bunches of flowers in his hand. He handed the carnations to Laura, who kissed him on the cheek and thanked him. Mia was presented with twenty-four beautiful roses, twelve red, and twelve white. She was taken aback, and her eyes welled up with unshed tears. She reached up and kissed him. Laura could tell Mia was overwhelmed, so she ushered everyone into the sitting room.

"Let me take your coat, Brian. What would you like to drink, wine, or beer?"

"A glass of wine would be lovely." Brian nodded at Max as he poured him a glass. "Thank you," he said.

They sat down to a lovely meal, which they all enjoyed. Laura had produced lamb shanks in a mint sauce dressing, with crispy roast potatoes and mixed vegetables.

"It's a shame Sam isn't home yet. He loves this meal," Mia proclaimed.

"Never mind, I'll cook it for him every day if he wants. I can't wait to get him home, and I'm glad he's not going back to nursery." Sam would not be able to go back for four weeks, and the nursery would have broken up for the holidays by then. He would be going to the local primary school in September, so Laura was looking forward to having him all to herself. Max was still going to physiotherapy sessions, and still had two months before he returned to work, so he could enjoy Sam's company, too.

When they were eating their desserts, Brian cleared his throat with a cough and asked, "Could I just say something, please?"

"Of course," Laura replied. "What is it?"

"I'd like to say thanks for a lovely meal and

such good company. However, I have something else to say tonight. I'm glad you're all here." Laura and Mia gave each other mystified looks. Brian looked hot under the collar, and moved his chair back. He dropped to one knee in front of Mia, and took her hand. He produced from his pocket, with much fumbling, a navy blue velvet box. By this time both girls knew what was coming and a tear slipped down Laura's face. She was so happy for Mia. She had never seen her look so radiant.

Before his courage evaporated, Brian gulped and said, "Mia, I love you. Please marry me!"

Mia jumped up, screaming, and pulled him to his feet with a strength she didn't know she had.

"Yes! Yes! Yes!" she shouted.

Laura was clapping, and Max was grinning from ear to ear. Brian swung Mia around and kissed her full on the mouth. He was usually very shy in front of everyone.

"I want you to come with me in the morning to look at some houses."

"I can't!" Mia cried. "I'm busy. Oh, dear – I just can't, Brian, any other time Brian, but not tomorrow morning." Brian saw the look of dismay on Mia's face.

"Ok, don't worry. We can go on Wednesday, if that's ok with you."

"Yes, that'll be fine. Laura and I are busy in the morning. It's personal, so we can't go into it."

"That's ok, love." Brian was grinning.

"What are you looking so smiley about, then?"

"I'm just letting it sink in that you said yes." They all laughed. "Come on, everyone," he went on. "Let's open some more wine."

"You can stop over if you want, Brian," Laura offered.

"No, that's fine, thanks. I need to be level-headed. I'll swap my day off for Wednesday, so I'll need to ring in first thing to see if it's ok."

Bonnie had watched the meal and kept quiet.

175

She didn't want to change the atmosphere. She was enthusiastic about tomorrow. It had been hard work for Rob to control her. He had travelled with her to all her favourite places. She knew she wouldn't be visiting them for a long time.

She wished she could have her time again, just to appreciate the places she took for granted. There was a lovely rose bush outside her old college: it had always been there. She had stood with Rob and marvelled, looking closely at the colours and the unique beauty of each petal. They seemed to glow. It was pure beauty that she had been too busy to notice when she was alive.

Rob told her that people do need to stop and notice the world around them. "Wherever you are, and however awful the place seems, beauty can still be found if only you stop to look."

Bonnie now knew what he meant, but it was too late for her now. She hoped the girls, after their visit, would understand more and have their lives enriched when they returned.

CHAPTER 16

The next morning Max left early to fetch some toys that Sam had asked him for when they had visited the toyshop before the accident. There was a Superman and a Spiderman figure, a dressing up suit of Spiderman and pyjamas that he wanted. Max would have purchased everything his little boy wanted, but he knew Laura and Mia would challenge him, so he stuck to the figures and dress up suit. Next week he would buy him the pyjamas. Once he had his purchases, he made his way back to the house. He was going to spend the morning with Sam, as Bonnie had told him to. He didn't mind: he loved his son; but he wondered what was going on, and whether Laura would tell him about it. He wouldn't push her: if she wanted to tell him, she would. He felt their excitement last night at the meal. They were both in an animated mood.

Max had a strange feeling. It was about Bonnie leaving, because of the visit he had received from her.

He grabbed the large holdall from the hall. He was going to put all Sam's clothes and toys in it – the ones he had been given at the hospital and the new ones he was taking him. Sam wanted to bring home every painting and drawing he had done while he was there. Max didn't care, as long as he got him home. He would be back by two in the afternoon – he'd see what mood the girls were in then.

Laura and Mia had their breakfast. They said goodbye to Max, then collapsed on the sofa with trepidation about the forthcoming event.

"I can't believe what's going to happen," Laura said.

"I know," Mia replied. "The pleasure of seeing mom again will kill me, I think."

Laura laughed aloud. "I know. I'm almost scared to death." Mia started laughing too, and soon they were rolling around on the settee, clutching their bellies, laughing at their own wit.

They stopped laughing, and both noticed at the same time that they were nervous. Both of their hands were shaking and their laughter sounded false even to their own ears.

"My tummy is rolling over" Mia said.

"Don't worry mines gone down the road," Laura laughed.

"I can't sit still and my heart is beating so fast like I've just done an hour in the gym" Mia was flushed and drips of perspiration were rolling down her head and dripping off the end of her nose.

Laura laughed and gave her a tissue.

"Let's just sit and wait. What time did they say?" Laura asked.

"Rob told us about nine-thirty," replied Mia.

They both slumped down on the settee and waited.

"I can't stand the waiting"

"I feel the same now sit still"

The clock seemed to be going slow on purpose and the ticking sound did nothing to alleviate their nerves.

Bonnie and Rob arrived at nine-thirty exactly. Bonnie spoke first, in a whisper so as not to panic Laura – though she jumped anyway, and started shaking from head to foot, which made Mia even more nervous. Rob placed a hand on each of their shoulders to calm them, and they both started to feel sedated.

Rob spoke, watching both girls for their reaction.

"It's going to be a very special day today, girls. Are you ready?" Laura told Mia what he had said, and they both replied "Yes" at the same time.

"Well, the first thing is that you'll be able to see and hear Bonnie and myself from this moment on."

They both gasped, and Bonnie spoke.

"Hello, Mia," she said.

Mia squeaked, "Hello." She started crying, and Bonnie put her arms around her. She felt it, and turned. Bonnie was standing in front of her.

"Oh, my goodness," she gasped. "I can see you ... your hair ... you have your hair!" she cried. Mia went white all the blood drained from her face and she collapsed in a heap on the sofa.

"Mia come on" Laura patted her sisters face until her eyes fluttered.

Mia came round and looked at Bonnie. "It was the hair. Oh Bonnie you are so beautiful"

The last time they had seen her she had lost all her hair because of the chemotherapy. Tears trickled down her cheeks. She couldn't control herself. She touched Bonnie, and felt her: it was as though she was alive. Laura stepped forward and did the same. Bonnie put both her arms around the girls, and they all hugged.

"Ahemmmm." They all turned to see Rob. Laura and Mia both gasped in astonishment – they could see him too. He was smiling down on them. His eyes were a piercing blue, and he was so tall that they both had to look up to him. He must have been at least six feet four inches tall. He was very handsome, and he glowed brightly as if he was lit up inside.

"Wow!" Laura exclaimed.

Rob burst out laughing, "I'll take that as a compliment."

Mia sat down in amazement. She was starting to feel faint again. She thought to herself that this was all too much to take in.

"I suppose this is the time, then," she said, looking first at Bonnie and then at Rob.

"Yes, my dear, the time has come."

"Can you just explain how and what and when?" Mia's jumbled sentence came pouring out so fast that she was almost choking on her words. Rob touched her again, and she started to breathe more evenly.

"Yes, I'll explain." Rob sat on the edge of the sofa while the girls sat holding each other. Laura and Mia could hardly take their eyes off Bonnie. They took in every contour of her face to commit to memory her lovely eyes and rosy lips. She was always beautiful. She looked even more so now, with her hair long and silky-brown. She looked amazing.

Rob let them take in the scene for a moment, then spoke.

"We'll all hold hands, my dears, and we'll travel. When we arrive, you will have your visit, and when I say it's over it will be over. You'll find yourselves back here on the sofa. You'll be very tired and in need of sleep. You won't see, feel or hear myself or Bonnie for a long while, but it may not be the end. And you'll need to go on living a normal life."

"Ok," Mia whispered. "We're ready, aren't we Laura?" Laura looked up into Bonnie's face and saw a sparkle in her eyes. "Yes," she said, turning to Mia. "We're ready."

CHAPTER 17

All four of them stood holding hands in the middle of the room. Laura and Mia felt a warm wind under their feet, and then they were lifted up. All of a sudden, they both looked up and saw light, lots of it, in various, and unusual colours. It was unlike anything they had ever seen before. It was incredible. The beauty of it humbled them. They could hear music, an angelic sound, like a choir of angels welcoming them.

They knew they would never hear such beautiful music again. Laura felt as though she was swirling in a never-ending vortex. As they travelled, they felt more love flowing into them. It was like the best kind of healing drug. The inner peace they felt as they travelled was indescribable.

They both watched in wonder as the colours constantly changed. They had never seen such stunning colours before. All of a sudden, there were a million sparking lights wrapped in a blanket of feathers. The feathers were translucent, with a neon blue glow. It was as though they were bouncing off the women. They enveloped them.

"How this could be?" Mia said out loud. The softest feeling they had ever felt was overwhelming them. The delicate feathers brushed past their legs and swirled around their feet.

Mia had not yet arrived, but already felt as though she didn't want to leave. Laura felt the same.

 "I'm happy with the journey, even without going any further." Mia said. The feeling of love was still seeping into their skin as they travelled. The love was so strong, and getting stronger.

"This experience is beyond words." Replied Laura as she felt herself twisting and turning.

Feeling they were arriving somewhere, they held their breaths. It was as though they had stepped out of a light. They were all standing on a beach, and Mia looked up at Rob.

"That was amazing. I'll remember that journey for the rest of my life."

"Yes Rob, that was phenomenal," Laura added. "It was stunning."

"Well," said Rob, "I didn't have to take you this way. We could have just arrived, but I wanted you to have the experience."

"Thank you." Laura put her hand up and touched Rob's cheek. "Thank you so much, you've been wonderful, and I'll be forever grateful to you for this."

"It's my pleasure," beamed Rob. His face went a deep crimson and Laura laughed "A big tall spirit like you getting embarrassed."

Rob smiled "Don't be cheeky or I'll take you back"

"Ok I I'm sorry" Laura said linking her arm through his.

The girls could hardly believe the peace they were both feeling. It showed on their faces, and

Bonnie asked them if they were feeling it.

"Oh yes," Laura replied.

Mia said, "its triple the feeling you gave me, Bonnie, when you touched me."

Rob put his arms around all three of them of them, and gave them a squeeze.

"This is only halfway heaven, remember."

Laura linked arms with Bonnie. "Oh my gosh, you have a lot to look forward to, Bonnie. How amazing."

The love was rippling through the girls' bodies in waves.

"I sure hope I can keep some of this love, Bonnie," Laura said..

"I'm sure Rob will let me bring you some in an emergency."

All three girls glanced at Rob. He looked horrified.

"Now look here, my dear, I've been more than patient with you." Bonnie laughed, and told him she was joking. Rob looked relieved, but gave her a stern look.

Bonnie touched Mia and Laura together, and looked deep into their eyes.

"I will love you both for ever. Thank you for having Sam." She kissed both of them on the cheek, and then she pointed to the far end of the beach. In the distance, a figure was approaching them. Both girls started weeping: they knew who it was immediately and squeezed each other's hands. Mia started walking, and then began to run, her hair flowing behind her. Laura hesitated for a moment, and then stumbled forward into a run. Mary ran towards them both. Her face was alight with love and affection. She was beaming. They all collapsed together, hugging and kissing each other. Laura couldn't believe it. They could feel her and hear her it was as though she was still alive. She looked so well, with rosy cheeks like the ones they remembered. The last time they had seen her was in the chapel of rest, and she had looked like a waxwork. That had given Mia nightmares for two weeks. Laura had returned and put make-up on her mother and made her look more like herself, but Mia had flatly refused to go back.

"My girls, oh, my girls," Mary exclaimed, kissing them in turn. "You're wonderful children. I love you with all my heart." Bonnie had stayed back to let her sisters have Mary to themselves, but Mary beckoned her over.

"Come here, Bonnie – all my three girls together. Let's walk." They strolled along the beach, all linking arms. It was a blissful moment they would never forget.. Laura laughed aloud, and Mary asked why.

"I was just thinking to myself, mom, that this is heavenly." They all laughed. Rob sat on a rock, watching the proceedings. He knew exactly how much time they had, and would give them only a moment's notice for a final hug and kiss. There would be no arguments.

Mary told them how she had felt when she first arrived, and how shocked she was.

"The only thing that made me stay was the love I felt here. I saw a window, and I was watching everyone."

The girls looked at each other in bewilderment.

"Why couldn't you speak like Bonnie?" Mary lowered her head in anguish.

"I'm not sure. I did try. I even sat on the end of your bed one evening, Mia, when you were having a nightmare. I couldn't communicate, and I'm sorry about that." Mia looked at her mom, and her eyes were sad.

"Don't be sorry, mom. I would have died if I'd heard you." Mary and Laura both grinned, and Mia realised what she had said.

"Oh dear, I'm going to be doing this a lot, I think."

Strolling along the beach it was so peaceful: no wonder their mother loved it here. It was delightful. The sea was a shimmering aqua blue and there was no wind – just a soft, warm breeze, which played with the stray hairs around their faces.

"Do any other spirits come here on the beach?" Laura enquired. Mary laughed out loud. Both the sisters remembered that laugh so vividly that they gasped.

"Oh yes, girls, hundreds of people come here. Come here, hold my hands."

Looking over towards Rob, Mary asked, "Do we have enough time, Rob?"

Rob nodded his head. "Yes you've got a little while longer."

"Good – now hold tight." The next thing the sisters knew, they were sitting on a large rock with their feet dangling over the edge into the water. Real water! It was dripping off their toes. They could actually feel the water in a rippling stream, and see fish swimming under the surface. The water was bright blue. Mary pointed towards a clump of reeds and shouted, "Look, girls." They all looked over and saw an otter playing with her babies.

"How can this be, mom? It's like we're on earth," said Mia.

"Remember girls, questions are for when you pass over, not for now. I just wanted to show you there are many places I can visit. I often visit Africa. I like to watch the lions and elephants."

Laura gasped. "You're having us on!"

Mary smiled. "Yes, I'm joking – but I could go there if I wanted to. Now come." She told them to join hands. "We'll go back to the beach" and with that they found themselves transported back.

Rob came towards them and they all held each other tightly. They knew what was coming.

"It's time, girls – you must return now."

Laura and Mia were weeping openly. Mary held them both close.

"Remember how much I love you, girls. Bonnie and I will be watching you, and you never know, we may visit you at any time." Bonnie smiled at them. She looked so beautiful.

"Look after Sam for me, please. I love you all so much. Please don't be sad, now you've seen where we are."

"Ready girls?" Rob said.

They weren't ready, but had no choice. All of a sudden, they were spinning again, very slowly, with gleaming colours spiralling from the tops of their heads to the tips of their toes. The colours were radiant.

"This is phenomenal," Mia said. Laura started to laugh and cry at the same time.

"There are no words to describe this – I'll never, ever forget it."

They both opened their eyes, and found themselves back on the sofa in Laura's house. They looked at each other, bewildered. Both their faces were soaking wet. Mia put her hand up, and Laura clasped it. They linked fingers and sat in silence for a few minutes. As they went to stand up, Laura pointed to the floor by their feet. Mia bent down and picked up four white feathers. They were so delicate, with an unearthly softness.

"I'll frame these with a picture of mom and Bonnie."

Laura was struck dumb, and just nodded. They were both full of emotion, and sat wordlessly for a while. Finally, Laura jumped up.

"Well, come on girl; let's get the house ready for when Sam comes back."

Mia followed her into the kitchen, smiling.

THE END

To be continued?

Lightning Source UK Ltd.
Milton Keynes UK
UKOW052207220212

187767UK00001B/22/P

9 781908 603517